FROM USA TODAY BESTSELLING AUTHOR

ERIN BEDFORD

TEMPTED BY THE *Butler*

HOUSE OF DURAND

BOOK FIVE

Also by Erin Bedford

The Underground Series
Chasing Rabbits
Chasing Cats
Chasing Princes
Chasing Shadows
Chasing Hearts
The Crimes of Alice
Hatter's Heart
Cheshire's Smile

The Mary Wiles Chronicles
Marked by Hell
Bound by Hell
Deceived by Hell
Tempted by Hell

Starcrossed Dragons
Riding Lightning
Grinding Frost
Swallowing Fire
Pounding Earth

The Crimson Fold
Until Midnight
Until Dawn
Until Sunset

Curse of the Fairy Tales
Rapunzel Untamed
Rapunzel Unveiled
Rapunzel Unchained

<u>Her Angels</u>
Heaven's Embrace
Heaven's A Beach
Heaven's Most Wanted

<u>House of Durand</u>
Indebted to the Vampires
Wanted by the Vampires
Protected by the Vampires
Embrace of the Vampires
Tempted by the Butler
Loved by the Vampires
Huntress of the Vampires

<u>Academy of Witches</u>
Witching On A Star
As You Witch
Witch You Were Here
Just Witch It
Summer Witchin'

<u>Children of the Fallen</u>
Death In Her Eyes
Fire In Her Blood

<u>House of Van Helsing</u>
Her Cross To Bear

The Beast of the Fae Court
Granting Her Wish
Vampire CEO

FROM USA TODAY BESTSELLING AUTHOR

ERIN BEDFORD

HOUSE OF DURAND
BOOK FIVE

Chapter 1
Piper

BULLSHIT. COMPLETE AND UTTER horse garbage. I've had to do a lot of stupid, meaningless jobs before but this one takes the cake.

I had to quit. I couldn't take it anymore. There was no way I was going to be able to handle doing this for the next, however fucking long I was going to be stuck here for. There was just nothing to it. I'd go insane first.

A whimper came from my feet, where I stood on the sandy beach of Seabrick.

"Don't look at me like that." I glared down at the six-inch Pomeranian that looked more like a scrubber brush than a dog. "You have no idea how much of a step down this is for me." I huffed and switched the leash into my other hand as I knelt down with my little plastic baggie to pick up Mister Fluffers' minuscule poop.

Mister Fluffers barked at me, wagging his tail.

"Cleaning toilets to picking up dog shit," I grumbled. "Yeah, that's a real step down."

Another bark was my answer.

"At least, I got orgasms with my job." I glared pointedly at Mister Fluffers. "You can't compete with that."

Mister Fluffers sat back on his heels and whined.

I rolled my eyes. "Don't give me those sad eyes. They don't work on me. I have much hotter men begging for my attention. I am immune to your charms."

The dog only whined more.

"Ugh!" I threw my hands up and knelt beside him, scratching behind his ears. "You know, you remind me of someone just as equally a pain in my ass."

"Are you talking to a dog?"

"Speak of the devil." I stood and brushed my hands on my shorts. "Have you come to keep an eye on me while I do my menial job?"

"You know, you don't need to do this job," Darren stepped up behind me, looking out of place on the beach in a full piece suit and gloves. "The Durands are still paying your salary."

I looked at him out of the corner of my eye. "You mean guilt money."

Darren sighed and lifted his eyes to the heavens, not arguing with me as he twisted his wrist to check his watch. He seemed to do that a lot lately. Not the looking up to the heavens bit - though he did do that too - the checking his watch bit.

Was Darren counting down the minutes until we could finally go home and stop hiding?

"I'm not taking money for a job I'm not doing anymore." I held my hand up before he could argue, the leash sliding down my wrist as I snapped at him, "And don't tell me that once a month counts which by the way, they have yet to keep to that promise."

"I wasn't-"

"Here." I shoved the baggie of poop at him.

Darren's nostrils flared but he took the bag regardless. He dropped it in a nearby trash can along Seabrick's only public beach and then gave me a pointed look. "As I was saying, I wasn't implying you were a whore but part of your job entails having to deal with certain extreme circumstances."

I snorted. "I wouldn't call hiding out in this sad town while the guys run for their lives an extreme circumstance. If I wanted to sit around on my ass all day, I could have done that back at home." I grimaced at the gritty feeling of sand between my toes. I probably shouldn't wear flip flops on the beach.

In any other circumstance, being stranded in Seabrick, a town of just over five thousand people with a fantastic view of the ocean, would be a dream come true. I could breathe in the air, and all I could taste was the salty sea. No pollution making you hack and cover your newly sensitive nose. There were a lot of benefits to being bound to a vampire but the extra olfactory senses I could have done without.

Thankfully, the beaches of Seabrick weren't overrun with tourists right now. I'd learned fast that crowds could be a bit overwhelming for my new senses. With the school year starting, Seabrick was entering its offseason, and we'd have several gloriously quiet months before the first break of the year came. I didn't plan on being here that long.

"If you do not like it here, I can bring it up to Master Durand when we speak next." Darren walked alongside me entirely at ease while people stared at him. Despite the fact that he was wearing a perfectly pressed and steamed suit, Darren was a looker. He would get stares anyway, even in jeans.

I snorted. Yeah, like that'd happen.

"What now?" Darren's lips turned down.

"You know it's eighty degrees out, right?" I jerked at Mister Fluffers' leash when the littler fucker tried to take off after another dog three times his size.

"So?"

I frowned at Mister Fluffers as he tried once more to attack the larger dog. "I'm just saying, you can wear something other than a suit. It's not like you're waiting on anyone now. You might think about getting a pair of shorts."

Darren arched a brow at me.

"Okay. Fine. Jeans. A pair of jeans wouldn't kill you. It would definitely draw less attention to - Mister Fluffers!" I stopped and glared at the ball of fluff. "That dog's poop is bigger than you. Do you want to die?" I huffed as Mister Fluffers barked at me, throwing my hands up in the air. "I give up. This job ain't worth it."

Darren smirked but said nothing.

I was determined to get a laugh out of the uptight butler. We'd only been in Seabrick for a few weeks, and he had the same stick up his ass as before. One would think that he'd have fewer responsibilities without Antoine around to bark orders. Still, while I was busy twiddling my thumbs, Darren was Antoine's liaison for all of their businesses. Apparently, Antoine couldn't run from vampire hunters and do business at the same time. Who knew?

"I'm starving," I said, at last, a bit more skip in my step now that I was dumping the dog walking job. "What do you feel like eating?"

"We could go order Frankie's-"

"No," I groaned, and grabbed my stomach. "No more Frankie's. I can't handle another corn dog." Who knew someone as classy as Darren was so obsessed with corn dogs? The guy could put back half a dozen corn dogs with no problem and still go back the next day.

"Very well, then where would you like to eat?"

I stared at the man curiously. His lower lip was pushed out, and his voice had a small, dejected sound to it. If I wasn't mistaken, Darren was pouting. I couldn't believe this man, who had several decades on me, was pouting about not getting to eat corn dogs for the third time this week.

Sighing in defeat, I hung my head. "Fine. If you really want Frankie's, we can go, but you have to explain to the others why I have an extra ten pounds on my ass next time they show up." I pointed at him with a stern look.

Darren's brows quirked as his eyes swept over my shorts and T-shirt clad form. "I don't know what you're referring to. You're always lovely."

I snorted. "Yeah, and you're a ray of fucking sunshine before you have your coffee. You forget we've been stuck living in the same room for several days now. I have no illusions of what kind of maniac I am, and neither should you."

Pursing his lips, Darren seemed to be trying to fight a smile. "Believe me. I have no such illusions, Piper Billings. I know exactly what kind of woman I am living with."

I didn't know if his words annoyed me or made me proud. Proud. Definitely proud.

"It's Durand now, remember?" I pointed out as Mister Fluffers barked in agreement.

"Of course. How could I forget?"

Chapter 2

Darren

"OF COURSE, MASTER," I answered into my cell phone. "I will be sure Mr. Chang is aware of the slight delay." I scribbled myself a note at the desk of the hotel room Piper and I shared. "Is there anything else, Master?"

There was a long pause on the other end of the phone before a puff of air. "How is she? Really?"

I glanced away from the paperwork before me and to the sleeping woman, not six feet away from me. Piper slept like a rag doll. Her arms thrown about the bed at all angles, her legs tangled up in the sheets. Small snores came from her mouth, which sat wide open, and a tiny bit of drool dripped from the edges of her lips.

My time here with Piper had been stressful and anxiety building. In all my time working for the Durands, I had never been put to the test in such a capacity. Before, I had only myself to worry about, and it is easy to hide one's self when they know the world they lived in.

Unfortunately, the world had become a larger place than the last time we had to evade the hunters. It wasn't so easy to duck into a barn and wait it out. Our every movement, every transaction, every telephone call was being tracked by someone, and it was just that easy for the hunters to tap into those as well.

"Darren?" Antoine's voice held a worry in it I hadn't heard in a while.

I remembered I didn't have long to speak to him before our call could be traced. Clearing my throat, I turned back to my desk. "Fine." I huffed a laugh and dragged my hand over my face. "Angry. Impatient. Needy."

Antoine chuckled a sound that sent a thrill through my body and hardened my cock beneath my slacks. "So, normal."

I nodded then remembered he couldn't see it. "Yes. Except Piper doesn't have an outlet to release her frustrations." And neither did I. I didn't add the last part, but our bond made sure that Antoine felt it.

"I cannot come just yet. They will be looking for me most of all." Antoine answered my unasked question. "Someone will come to help this week."

"She will be pleased." I placed my hand on top of my length, and pulled at it, willing it to behave.

We were silent for a breath before Antoine said, "I have to go."

"Of course."

"Go to the bathroom," his voice full of his commanding power I had no choice but to obey.

I stood from my chair ever so quietly and walked across the room to the minuscule but clean bathroom.

"Close the door."

My body quaked with the need to obey, and my cock hardened even more with each word. I waited for his next command, knowing I was not to do anything before he commanded it.

"Unzip your pants and touch yourself." Antoine's smooth dominating voice almost had me exploding right there. Except it wouldn't be half as delicious as what would happen next.

My fingers wrapped around the sensitive flesh and a hiss released from me.

"That's it." Antoine cooed, pleased with my actions. "Stroke yourself for me. We may be apart, but there's no reason you should go without."

Moving my hand up and down my shaft as he commanded, I gasped and leaned against the sink, trying to keep quiet. Piper had as good of hearing as I did, and if I could hear her touching herself in her bedroom across the hall, then she for sure would be able to hear me in the bathroom.

"Cup yourself," Antoine commanded, and I did as he asked with my other hand, tugging on my aching cock. "Now," he pushed even more power into his voice this time, and I almost collapsed to my knees at the effort. "Remember what it was like to be deep inside of our little maid's pussy."

I gasped at his words, surprised and even more turned on.

"So warm," he purred into the phone, and my mind filled with the image of Piper sitting on the edge of Antoine's desk. Her legs spread wide for me. "She felt good, didn't she? Wrapped tightly around your cock. So wet."

I grunted.

"What was that?" Antoine growled.

"Yes," I gurgled, my thumb flicking over the head of my cock as I tried to hold back my release until commanded.

"Now isn't that nice? If I hadn't stopped you that night but joined you? I could have fucked your perfect ass while you fucked our mouthy little maid." Antoine seemed almost angry as he said it, but I didn't release myself to placate him. I was his to command, and if this was what he wanted, then I would be more than happy to oblige.

I felt myself on the edge. Ready to burst at any moment. I moaned into the phone. "Please, Master. I can't-"

"You may cum."

Those three words were all I needed. My body tightened, and my eyes squeezed closed as a dam broke and hot liquid spurted all over my hand. I held the phone against my ear with my shoulder, almost dropping it in the moment of release. My legs buckled beneath me as I sank to the floor.

"Thank you, Master," I murmured into the phone almost a sigh of relief.

"Perhaps, one day, we can make that little fantasy a reality," Antoine said it so matter of fact, as if he had already decided it himself. I didn't want to incur his wrath the way I had before with Piper, so I stayed silent, my breathing the only sound coming through the phone.

"I will call again." The call ended. Nothing about when he would call again only that he would. While Antoine could feel what Piper and myself were feeling, we were not given the same. This was one of those times I wished I knew what he was thinking.

Had I angered him in some way? Was the fantasy he played out supposed to be a test? And if so, had I passed or failed it?

I went about cleaning up the mess I made and quickly showered, making sure to clean any residual of my activities from my body. I didn't know why I tried to hide it. It wasn't as if Piper didn't know I masturbated. Though strangely, I hadn't caught her doing the same.

Back at the manor, she had no qualms with touching herself, even when she knew the others could hear her. Not that she had known of my abilities at that time. I doubted it would have stopped her. It was what made her restraint now so queer.

I stepped out of the shower and dried off, wrapping a towel around my waist as I entered the bedroom. My gaze darted to Piper's sleeping form. This time she had her back to the door, and her breathing was slightly erratic.

Had she heard?

Not wanting to embarrass her, I set about dressing for bed. My gaze kept moving to her back, tense and no doubt feeling my eyes on her.

If Antoine's fantasy had been a test, I had surely failed it.

I was not a homosexual man who only craved the flesh of other men. I have been with women before with Antoine and without. We have never defined our relationship as one in which we were exclusive only to each other.

However, with Piper now, it was different. Antoine was different.

He was possessive, and yet he wanted to share her with his brothers. Antoine both enjoyed her flesh and wanted me to as well. Except he seemed to be at war with himself. A war Piper and I were in the middle of.

Only time would tell if whatever was causing the conflict would resolve itself or if we would get the brunt of the backlash.

"Good night, Piper," I murmured into the room as I settled into my bed.

A slight catch of her breath told me she was indeed awake. There was silence for several heartbeats as my eyes grew heavy before a small voice replied back, "Good night, Darren."

Chapter 3
Piper

"IF YOU BURY YOUR face any further in your coffee, you're going to drown, Dear," Trudy, the waitress at Just A Cup, frowned at me from across the bar top counter.

I lifted my face slightly and smiled politely. "Thanks."

Just A Cup had been my safe haven since Darren and I were whisked away from everything we knew to hideout. Darren kept spouting out rules and was getting on my last nerve. That was when I found this little slice of heaven. The coffee was good and hot, and their pastries weren't bad either. I was sure I'd be gaining a few extra pounds if I kept indulging myself, but I just couldn't seem to care. They were worth it.

Trudy leaned on the counter in between us, her ample bosom threatening to pop the buttons of her baby pink shirt. "I know I only met you a few weeks ago, but I've never seen you so distraught. What's on your mind?"

I liked Trudy. She didn't wear too much makeup, and she knew when I wanted to be left alone or when I needed to talk. Trudy had kind blue eyes and bright red hair that couldn't possibly be natural, but the streaks of white coming through at her hairline said otherwise. She was everything I thought a mother should have been. Everything my mother wasn't. Plus, she had coffee. Just that small bit would have made me like her more than my own mother.

"I'm alright." I forced my head entirely up to meet her gaze. "Just thinking."

Trudy reached over and grabbed the coffee pot nearby, filled my cup and pushed the creamer and sugar in my direction. "Trouble at home?"

I dropped my eyes to my cup, busying myself with making the bitter liquid tolerable.

I couldn't look Darren in the face this morning. I had darted out of the bedroom the moment I woke up. I barely stopped to put on a bra and my flip flops, let alone check to see if he was awake before I left. I still wore my tank top and shorts from bed.

Thankfully, Trudy didn't judge.

"I know a woman who's avoiding someone when I see one." Trudy gazed pointedly at my haphazardly put up hair.

Okay, so maybe she does judge.

My face heated. Remnants of last night filling my ears.

Antoine calling out commands over the phone. Darren making small groaning sounds, trying, but failing to be quiet so I didn't overhear him.

If I had been an average human, I wouldn't have even woken up, but ever since Antoine marked me, I hadn't gotten a decent night's sleep. Everything woke me up. The creaking of the floorboards. The owl in a tree a few houses down. There was no way I wouldn't have heard Darren with only a wall between us.

It made a girl wonder. Had he wanted me to hear? Darren was a hard man to read. As far as I could tell, the butler hadn't changed any of his feelings toward me, even after the incident with Antoine a few months ago. Darren wasn't casting longing looks at me. He wasn't finding excuses to touch me. In fact, if anything, he was keeping his distance more than ever.

"It's just," I sighed and sat my cup down, rubbing my forehead with my fingers. "We have a dynamic between us, and things have gotten...complicated." I tried my best to explain without giving away too much information.

"Isn't it always?"

Trudy thought Darren and I were here for work. Checking out the area for future work endeavors. I'd insisted we were just work colleagues, but I didn't think she believed me. Maybe it was because we were sharing a hotel room. Perhaps because Darren acted like a possessive boyfriend whenever he came in. Standing just a hint too close, his eyes scanning the cafe as if a vampire hunter was going to jump out and snatch me in broad daylight.

"So, what happened?" Trudy prodded, not giving up on getting it out of me.

"Don't you have other customers to interrogate?" I glanced around the cafe and noticed the utter lack of customers. I pursed my lips and huffed. "I'm already involved with someone else. Our boss, actually."

Trudy arched a brow. "But your boss, the one you're involved with, sent you off alone with that handsome man? Is he broke in the noggin' or something?"

I smirked. "Or something."

"So, what's the problem? You havin' feelings for this Darren fellow now instead of your boss?"

I shifted in my seat. "No. I mean, not like that. I don't know." I pulled on my ponytail and sagged in my chair. "We had a moment -" More than a moment, I felt him inside of me "- a few months ago, and it's kind of changed things."

Trudy smiled knowingly. "You mean, you're noticing things about him that you wouldn't have before this 'moment' happened."

I nodded. "Yeah, and living so close together isn't helping matters. I can't do my job like this, and I don't want to be unfaithful to...my boss."

"Is this boss more attractive? Have a lot of money?" Trudy cocked her head to the side, interest lighting her eyes.

I shrugged a shoulder. "They're both about the same in looks, I guess. Obviously, our boss has more money. But it's not about that."

"What is it then?"

"I don't want to be that girl," I began, looking at her pointedly. "The one who can't be faithful unless her man is around all the time. We were assigned here without knowing how long we would be here or when we'd get to go back. Plus, he's off...doing business elsewhere. He might never come back."

"Do you love him?" Trudy asked abruptly. "In my experience, love is worth waiting for, but if you don't..."

Pausing for a long moment, I stared hard at my coffee. Did I love Antoine? It was hard to say. Could I love more than one person? If not, then was I wrong to keep them all? That didn't necessarily mean I loved Darren either. I was just feeling...weird.

"Then, give yourself a break." Trudy pushed off the counter and nodded. "You're in an impossible situation. Anything can happen, and until they do, don't stress. You'll get wrinkles." She winked at me before turning to go help a customer who had just entered.

"Don't stress," I muttered to myself as I sipped from my cup and then snorted. "Yeah. Like that was going to happen."

Chapter 4

Darren

PIPER'S BED LAID EMPTY in the morning. At first, a moment of panic set it at seeing her discarded blankets and her purse gone. Piper was as quiet as a Rhino in a china shop. Most mornings, I woke to her trampling around the room, opening and shutting drawers without a care to waking me up.

She didn't so much as make a sound today. Either I slept harder than usual, or she hadn't wanted to wake me.

I couldn't imagine why.

Seeing as Piper's phone was also missing, I didn't bother going after her. If she needed time alone, then I would give it to her. Living this close to one another in such a small space after having a whole mansion to run through has put its toll even on me. I like my space. My quiet. I missed my bed and my nightly routine.

I could still manage now, but it wasn't the same. I couldn't unwind the way I could back home with a cup of tea and a nice book. Some nights even sitting by the fire. Though, the Georgia weather was too warm most days to need one.

Surprisingly, I found myself missing the kitchen. While Gretchen cooked the majority of nights, I would give anything for even a hot plate to make a decent cup of tea rather than this instant type that was either too hot or too cold for a proper cup of tea. Though, there was a lovely cafe down the street that had the closest thing to a good cup of coffee I could get in this town.

Deciding on where I would go first before I began my work for the day, I busied myself dressing. The room we stayed in had an ironing board and iron but nothing so fancy as the one I had back home. I couldn't even make a proper pleat in my slacks. I have tried to make do with what I had, not wanting to risk exposing where we were hiding just because of my preferences. Now that we have been here for a few weeks, I could finally find a dry cleaner of some kind to take care of my clothing.

I adjusted my suit jacket and buttoned the cufflinks, sniffing as I thought of what Piper would have said to my choice of clothing.

She'd say I looked ridiculous and should just give in and buy a pair of jeans already.

Jeans. I snorted. As if I would ever wear something so common.

Even if I didn't have this position, serving in Antoine's stead, I couldn't wrap my head around wearing something so confining. So rough in material.

My cell phone pinged. Picking it up, I glanced at the screen.

Antoine messaged me.

Nice.

I deleted the message immediately and placed my phone in my front left pocket.

So, they were heading to Nice next. It'd be a while before they could get over here to visit. I didn't agree with Antoine's bouncing back and forth between countries. It was an unnecessary risk to themselves using the jet. Still, I knew better than to voice my opinion on the matter. Antoine would do whatever he saw fit to protect this family. I had to do my part, keeping the businesses intact and keeping Piper in check.

I glanced around the empty hotel room and sniffed.

My ability to do that was sorely lacking.

Tucking my wallet into my pocket, I headed out to find my missing coworker.

I strode down the hallway toward the foyer. The slight tinge of mildew filled the air. No doubt they had tried to remove the smell with multiple cleaners, but it would not get past my heightened sense of smell.

The maroon carpet had brown and gold decorative lines meant to help hide any spills or stains without extensive cleaning. I had used the same tricks myself to hide messes when the masters became overzealous. Thankfully, the walls of the hotel were a cream color, bringing some form of light into the area else it would feel as if one were in one of those horror films.

The Chaucer Hotel was quaint to be polite. With only a dozen or so rooms, it was one of the smaller hotels available in Seabrick. It didn't get a lot of tourist traction. Those who were still here past the tourist season were for business or those visiting families. It made it easier for Piper and me to blend in as business ventures ourselves.

I chose it for those reasons and more. Though Piper would have had us stay in one of the more luxurious hotels, this wasn't my first time hiding out, and I doubted it would be my last. We would have to make do until it was safe.

If only I could keep Piper out of trouble until that time.

"Mr. Durand, good morning." The woman, Madeline, who worked the front desk most mornings, offered me a bright, almost flirtatious smile. She kept it professional for the most part, but she hadn't tried very hard to hide her attraction to me.

"Good morning," I offered back with a polite smile. "Have you seen my companion?"

While nothing was going on between Piper and myself, I never let it seem as if I were available. Calling Piper my companion versus my coworker or friend put that level of uncertainty into our relationship. It was a trick that I had to use during vampire politics as well. One never knew who might be waiting to take a bite out of you regardless of your blood bond.

Madeline's smile wilted, but she pushed it back into place and nodded. "She left as I came in for the morning." Her brows furrowed. "I might give her a little space."

"Oh?"

"I haven't known you two very long, but I do know women, and Piper was not a happy camper this morning." She offered me a sympathetic smile.

I returned it. "Is she ever?"

Giggling like a schoolgirl, Madeline covered her mouth with her hand and ducked her head. "I suppose not."

Nodding my head in thanks, I started for the door before pausing. "Did you happen to see which way she went?"

Leaning on her elbow and beaming up at me, she shrugged a shoulder. "The only place in town you can brood before ten o'clock."

"Of course, my thanks." Stepping out the door, I turned to the left toward the only decent place to get a cup of coffee in a fifty-mile radius.

Piper went on and on about how there wasn't a decent commercialized place for coffee in this Podunk town, as she called it. She made me go all over town with her until we found a cup of coffee worth the bean it was made from.

That place ended up being Just A Cup. A little mom and pop cafe that had an apple pie that could rival even Gretchen's.

It didn't take me long to get to the cafe. Unfortunately, a second after stepping in the door, I knew Piper wasn't there. Trudy was, though.

She turned from her current customer to smile in my direction. Her plump form cocked to one side as she waved a hand toward the bar chair. "You already missed her, gorgeous. Why don't you sit on down and I'll get you a cup and a piece of pie."

A genuine smile touched my lips. "You are wasted here, Trudy. I'm half tempted to have my employers give you an offer you can't refuse." I unbuttoned my jacket and sat in the offered chair and waited for her to finish with her customer.

When Trudy could turn her attention entirely to me, she slid a plate of pie in front of me with a large scoop of ice cream on top. The only place I knew that had no problem serving me pie before lunch. I'd have to make sure it was something that I kept up when we returned home.

"Now, sugar," Trudy poured steaming liquid into my cup and stood back, watching me, "What's going on with you and your old lady."

I smirked against my coffee cup. "She's not my wife."

Shrugging, Trudy sat the coffee pot down nearby. "Married or not. You might as well be with the way you two have been carrying on lately."

I arched a brow. "Whether or not that is true, she's promised to another."

"Your employer," Trudy stated instead of asking. "Yeah, I heard about this so-called employer who sent his girl away with a catch like you and hasn't bothered to check in. Sounds like he doesn't much care for either of you."

My jaw tightened as I drank from my cup. "I assure you that is not the case."

"Whatever you say, dearie." She refilled my cup with a motherly smile. "Whatever you say."

Chapter 5
Piper

SIGHING, I LEANED MY face on my hand, pouring over the classified at a picnic table by the beach.

The paper had a total of five jobs for hire. Not that I should expect more in this town. I was lucky to have found the dog walking job as it was. The ones that were in the paper weren't much better.

Wanted: caregiver for an eighty-five-year-old man.

No, thank you. It was terrible enough cleaning up after dogs and vampires. I so did not want to wipe any butts.

Waitress for a burger joint down the street. Nope. Their burgers tasted like shit, and the staff was just as shitty.

I paused at the next listing. Now, this, this I could stomach. Not like I haven't done it before. Though, I suppose it would be a step back since I'd just gotten out of a job like this when I got hired by the Durands.

Okay. So, I got fired. But that was neither here nor there. Besides, I'm a different person now.

I could totally deal with some asshole lawyer shouting orders, answering meaningless phone calls, and making appointments. Of course, I'd have to wear something professional for a lawyer's office. I couldn't exactly wear what I cleaned the manor in. I smirked. Well, what I usually wore to clean around the house anyway. Though, I didn't think this Bigg's Law Office would require me to play hostess to a thousand-year-old vampire.

A shadow fell over my form. I resisted the urge to roll my eyes.

"If you are going to make an escape, at least leave a note. Or text. That's what cellular devices are for."

I didn't bother looking up at Darren as I circled the receptionist's job in the paper. I'd make up a resume and email it to them tonight. Or better yet, I'll take it to them in person. I've been told I can be charming...when I want to be. I certainly had to have a certain amount of charm to attract five vampires to me.

I chuckled to myself.

"Something funny?"

Lifting my head up, I smiled at Darren. "Yes. It is. What do you want?"

Darren sighed, his brow pinched in that way it did when he was annoyed with me but was too polite to say so. "You've been avoiding me."

"No, I haven't." I glanced back down at the paper focusing on folding it into a perfect square around the job I'd circled. "I've been busy."

"Looking for a job?" Darren unbuttoned his suit jacket and sat on the bench next to me. "You know you put us at an unnecessary risk every time you go off on your own like this."

I turned my head to the side. "And I'm supposed to just live in fear? Stay in the hotel room until Antoine says that it's safe again?" I shoved the newspaper into the side of my bra through my tank top. "Not going to happen."

"I'm not saying sequester yourself in the hotel room. I'm saying you need to be more careful." He adjusted his white gloves so precisely that I had the urge to push him down in the sand just to see him all ruffled and distraught.

"I am being careful."

Darren snorted. "So, leaving the hotel room without telling me where you were going, without decent clothing, that's being careful? I wish I could say I was surprised you even took your cell phone but your generation..." he clucked his tongue impatiently, "...can't seem to be away from it for more than a moment. It'd be attached to your hand permanently if you could."

I did roll my eyes this time, standing. "Careful, your age is showing." I flicked his nose, gaining me a glower from Darren.

"Not as much as yours." He stood and adjusted his jacket, rebuttoning the middle button. A curious act I was sure was habit rather than need. "Are you done running?"

I cocked my head. "I'm not running. I'm standing right here."

"Don't be tart." He narrowed his dark eyes on me.

I stuck my tongue out at him. "I'll be whatever I want to be. You're not my boss."

"Thank god for that," he muttered under his breath, probably forgetting I could hear him.

I turned on my heels and practically skipped along the sidewalk by the beach. I hummed to myself envisioning what kind of clothing I'd need to wear to my new job. I frowned. I didn't have much money from the dog walking job. While I loathed spending the money, Antoine was no doubt still paying me - I hadn't checked my account in ages - I needed a better wardrobe than short shorts and tank tops.

"What's the job?"

I glanced up from the ground, pausing as a group of bikini-clad women passed by us. Their eyes locked on Darren, and they liked what they saw. My stomach shifted strangely. I pushed the feeling down and shook my head. "What?"

"The job you circled in the paper," Darren continued as if he hadn't seen the women leaving trails of drool in their wake.

"Oh," I jerked my eyes forward. "A receptionist for a lawyer's firm."

Darren frowned. "I thought you hated those kinds of jobs."

"No," I corrected him. "They didn't like me. I like them fine." I kicked the ground as we walked. "It'll be good for me. I'll get out of the hotel. You'll have more time for yourself to do work for Antoine and... other stuff." I bit the inside of my cheek, willing my face not to go red.

Darren quieted.

"Is that okay?" I stopped and looked at him.

He was staring at me strangely.

"What's wrong?" I angled my head to the side, then touched my face. "Did I get pen on my face?"

Shaking his head, Darren turned away from me. "No, you're lovely. Let's go find something to eat. Then perhaps we could see about getting you something to wear for your job interview."

I laughed. "I don't have the job yet. I haven't even applied."

Darren's lips ticked up at the edges. "I have no doubt you will charm them the same way you charmed the Durands."

Chapter 6
Darren

"PIPER STARTED HER NEW job today." I made sure to keep my tone even as Wynn sat across from me at the hotel room dining table. I didn't want to ruin this for her.

Wynn's brows rose, his blue eyes alighting with interest. "Really? And she didn't find her position with you here...fulfilling?"

He was laughing at me.

Forcing myself to relax, I crossed and uncrossed my legs as I lifted my teacup to my lips. "Can you blame her? Stuck in this room every day with nothing to occupy her time. This is your first visit. Perhaps, you will be able to quell her restless feet?"

Wynn snorted, lounging back in his chair. Even in hiding, he still acted like he did not have a care in the world. His black hair fell over his shoulders like waves, his silk shirt tight across his chest. The majority of the buttons of his shirt were undone, allowing the house sigil tattooed on his chest to be seen - a black crow on a branch surrounded by the Latin words. Each of the Durands had the tattoo.

Antoine had asked me once if I wanted to get one as well, but I declined. Someone had to be able to move around undetected in the human world. If I had the tattoo, then it would be easy for the other vampires to know I belonged to them.

"Nothing will quell that woman but a right smack to her pert ass." Wynn licked his lips, the edges curling up wickedly. "Even then, I'm not sure it would help." He chuckled, the sound causing a shiver to go through, making my cock harden slightly.

Taking a deep breath to push down the side effects of Wynn's abilities, I sat my cup down. "I cannot disagree with you there."

Wynn fiddled with his cup, long cold without being touched. "Where is our girl? A new job, you said?"

I inclined my head. "Yes, at a law firm. She's working as a receptionist."

The vampire across from me threw his head back and laughed. "Oh, please tell me you are joking. Piper? A girl who couldn't be proper if her life depended on it working in a stuffy law firm?"

"I don't see how it's funny." Piper snapped from the doorway. She stalked across the room, chunking her purse and phone on the table between us. "I am completely capable of being a proper human being."

"So, you can..." Wynn purred, his eyes eating up her appearance.

My gaze skimmed over Piper's attire. I'd seen her wearing it this morning but had a new appreciation for the tight black skirt that fitted her backside like a glove. Her blouse, the color of dried blood, was made of silk just like Wynn's. The humidity outside made the material stick to her like a second skin. It gave a tantalizing view of her cleavage.

"What are you doing here, Wynn?" Piper let out an exasperated sound, and while she tried to hide her annoyance at seeing him, something had shifted about her being. Her shoulders were more relaxed. Her expression was less tight. So, while her words said she didn't want to see him, her entire being said, she was relieved. Happy even.

"Why to see you, my love." Wynn took her hand in his, lacing their fingers together.

She tried to wiggle her hand away, but Wynn held tight. "There's such a thing called a phone."

I snorted. Piper glared my way.

"What am I missing?" Wynn inquired with an arched brow.

"Nothing," Piper bit out. "What do I owe your presence, and why you?"

Wynn grasped his chest with his free hand and mocked pain. "I am distraught. And here I thought you were pining after me all this time. Have I already lost your affections?"

Piper rolled her eyes and tugged her hand once more. "Stop it."

Giving her hand a good tug, Wynn pulled her into his lap. She put up a half-hearted fight but settled into his lap, almost with a sigh. His arms wrapped around her waist. "Tell me, my pet. Have I lost you? Do I need to hunt down this fiend who has captured your heart?" His words were low and teasing, his lips brushing along her cheek.

I lowered my gaze to my cup. "Did you have a message from Master Durand? An update on the situation?" My words came out harsher than I meant them to be, making me frown.

Wynn looked away from Piper long enough to answer me. "Nothing pertinent. Still on the run. Still no closer to finding the vampire hunters' hideout or how to get the bastards off our trail."

"What about Master Rayne?" I prodded, not giving him the chance to turn back to kissing up Piper's neck. "Do his computer skills fail him? Can he not forge some new papers? New identities."

"He has." Wynn's gaze narrowed on me, annoyance bunching his brows. "How do you think we have survived all these years? Our wits? Rayne has done everything he is able and then some, but we can't get the devil's hounds off our scent."

"There must be some way -"

"Enough," Wynn snapped, and I stiffened, everything in me demanded I kneel and ask for forgiveness. I fought against the need, gaining me a surprised but not angry look from Wynn.

Piper smacked Wynn on the chest, gaining his attention. "Knock the fuck off, will you? We're all on the same side. Darren wants answers just like I do. We're going bat shit crazy stuck in this place."

"Then, perhaps, I should help relieve you of some of your stress." Wynn purred once more, his attention solely on Piper. "I have missed you, love. Your scent, your smart mouth..." he kissed her. "Your taste." He moaned. "If I could bottle your flavor up and take it with me, I would."

Piper giggled and pushed him away. "You're such a freak."

"Only for you," Wynn murmured into her neck, the scent of blood tinging the air.

Piper didn't push Wynn away, her eyes rolling up as she clung to him. It was as if I didn't even exist.

I shifted away from the table and stood. "I believe I'll take a walk. Please take your time."

The gasps and moans filled my ears before I even made it out the door.

Chapter 7
Piper

A DOOR CLOSED SOMEWHERE nearby, but I couldn't pull myself out of the lust-filled fog Wynn had put me in from just his bite alone.

Later I'd ask why I was so easily taken over by his bite. Later, when I wasn't fighting to keep myself from rubbing all over Wynn like a cat in heat.

"Wynn," I moaned against the sharp pleasure of the fangs buried in my neck.

The hardness of his cock pressed against my backside. I wiggled against it, pushing myself against him. Wynn's hands tightened around my waist, one of them slipping up my back and cupping the back of my neck, angling my head back further. After a second more, he withdrew his fangs with a loud gasp of air. The hot touch of his tongue slid up and down my neck, healing the wound with his saliva.

"Your blood," Wynn groaned, licking his lips and brushing his fingers along the edges of it, sucking off the excess of my blood. My eyes were drawn to each movement, unable to look away for even a moment. "I will never find another who tastes so sweet."

I scrunched my nose up. "I'm not sure if that is a compliment..."

"Oh, it is my little maid." Wynn slipped his arms beneath my legs and lifted us.

I wrapped my arms around his neck and held on tight though I knew there was no need. Wynn would never drop me.

Then as if to spite my words, Wynn dropped me three feet above the bed. I startled squeal escaped me, and I was weightless for a brief millisecond. Then I bounced on the hard bed and collapsed in an annoyed bundle.

"You didn't have to do that." I leaned up on my elbows and glowered. "I could have walked."

Wynn crawled onto the bed, prowling toward me like a lion preying the gazelle. His fingers wrapped around my ankle, moving up each inch of my flesh and under my black skirt. His touch left a trail of fire in its wake. My thighs involuntarily pressed together in anticipation. When he reached as far as he was able to go, a loud rip followed by a gust of air had me scowling.

"I'll buy you ten new ones," Wynn purred, lifting one of my thighs, his lips brushing along the inside of my leg.

My breath hitched. "That's beside the point. I need the clothes I have for my new job."

A warm wet muscle licked my flesh, moving closer and closer to my pulsating center. "You already have a job," Wynn murmured hotly against my skin. "Right here...with me."

I lifted my eyes to the ceiling and shoved at his head, pushing him away. I threw my legs over the edge of the bed and gathered the remains of my skirt with a frown.

"What's wrong?" Wynn tried to reach for me. "Piper?"

I scooted away from his grasp and stood. "I'm not your property. You all think just because I work for you that I'm going to be at your beck and call." I stalked over to the dresser and grabbed out a pair of sleep shorts. Shoving one foot and then the other into them, I tied them with twitching fingers.

"Piper..." Long thin fingers gripped my shoulders and I tensed, itching to move away but knowing he would just follow after me. "Where's this coming from?"

Sighing deep, I wrapped my arms around myself. "Where's this going? All of us? I mean, I clean your house, and Darren does...well whatever Antoine tells him to do...but what does that mean? Am I going to be your maid forever?" I spun around and peered up at him. "Are we ever going to have a real relationship, or are you only going to come to me when you want sex?"

Wynn's brows drew together tight at my words and then, after a moment, relaxed as he smiled that gorgeous smile of his. "Is that what you're worried about?"

I let him wrap his arms around my waist and draw me near, his forehead pressed against mine. "Yes. Kind of. And other things."

"Well, we can worry about the other things later." Wynn grasped my hand with his and led me to the hotel door.

"Wait," I dug my feet into the carpet, trying to stop us. "Where are we going?"

"On a date, of course," Wynn smirked over his shoulder. "You're right, I have been a bit lax in the romance department, and that's something I plan to rectify now."

My eyes bulged. With all the strength I could muster, I yanked my hand from his grip. "You want to go on a date now? With me dressed like this?" I jerked a hand down at myself. "I don't think so."

"What?" Wynn scanned my form, from my short sleeping shorts to the silk of my button-down shirt. "You look lovely to me."

I snorted. "If I wore a dress of meat, you'd think I was lovely."

Wynn wagged his brows. "And delicious."

I rolled my eyes. "Let me change and then we can go find something for dinner." Wynn opened his mouth, and I cut him off. "Something that's not me."

Briefly, I thought about messaging Darren then thought better of it. I had just complained about not getting romanced, if I bring along someone else that would dismiss the whole point I was making.

"Very well, I will wait outside for you." Wynn inclined his head and headed for the door once more.

I went through the closet as the door closed behind me. We hadn't brought much with us to Seabrick. We couldn't go back to the house to get things when we left Bulgaria, running from the vampire hunters. What we had, Darren and I bought when we got here. Most of it from online retailers. I hadn't thought of buying many going out clothes. The only item I had splurged on was a short dark blue dress and I hadn't even taken the tags off of it yet.

Pulling it off the hanger, I disrobed and shimmied into the cool cloth, delighted at the feel of the material smooth against my skin. I grabbed one of the pairs of shoes I just bought for my new job. I couldn't very well wear flip flops to a law office. Thankfully, that meant I had something to wear for tonight.

My makeup was still done from work, but my hair needed a proper brushing through—damn vampire. I pursed my lips and dragged a brush through it.

When I was happy with my appearance, I grabbed my purse and headed for the door.

Wynn stood on the other side, sucking down on the bud of a cigarette.

I arched a brow. "When did you start smoking?"

Flicking the cigarette away, Wynn blew the smoke off to the side. "When you've lived as long as I have vices come and go." His gaze dipped to take in my dress. "Why, Piper, you look absolutely bitable."

I giggled. "I'm sure."

"Shall we," he offered me his arm.

Slipping my arm through his, I snuggled up to Wynn's side.

"What's good to eat in this town?"

Chapter 8
Darren

THERE'S ONE SINGLE BAR in Seabrick. The Croaking Parrot. Garish in decor, it at least offered a quiet place to think and a stiff drink.

"Another one?" The bartender behind the counter asked, fluttering her lashes at me in an attempt to flirt.

I nodded, pushing my empty tumbler toward her. "Make it a double."

The bartender, Trixie, giggled. "You're going to regret drinking on an empty stomach. Why don't I get you some wings to go with it? On the house."

I didn't respond, allowing her to make her own decision. I didn't want to eat. I wanted to drink. To forget the weird twisting sensation in my gut.

Why had seeing Wynn with Piper bother me so? It's not like they haven't kissed and more in my presence. The others included. There was nothing new about that.

So, why?

I thanked Trixie as she sat the tumbler in front of me. Sipping from the glass, I savored the scotch as it burned down my throat. Very few things were consistent in my time alive. Times change. As did tastes in clothing and music. One thing that never changes was a good scotch.

"You going to tell me what's got such a sexy man like yourself drinking here alone on a Thursday night?" Trixie leaned on the bar, pushing her chest against her arms in her attempts to tantalize me.

Long knowing to keep my troubles to myself, I sat my tumbler back on the bar. "Just enjoying a night on my own."

I hoped she would leave it at that.

Trixie giggled. "Well, I get off around two if you'd like some company?"

I didn't answer her, staring down into my drink.

Thankfully, another patron called her away, letting me sulk and drink alone.

As soon as the sunset, Wynn had appeared out of nowhere. Knocking on our hotel door as if he had every right to be there. Which he did. That didn't make it feel any less intrusive.

One would think I would be used to the Durands butting into my life. They'd been a shadow over me for the last few hundred years. Nothing has changed. So, I shouldn't feel any different about it now.

Except, I did.

I liked being on my own away from the manor. Even if it was with Piper.

In fact, I haven't broken away and gone out on my own in years. Antoine didn't forbid it. He encouraged it every century or so. It kept the lot of us from trying to kill one another.

However, in these modern times, it was safer to hide from those who would notice my inability to age when we were together.

People were nosy by nature. It was even worse now that you could find anything out about anyone online. It was one of the reasons Antoine had his finger in several industries. The humans he worked with would start to question things if they ever knew the truth.

The door to the bar opened, and my shoulders bunched. I didn't need to turn to know who had entered the bar.

"Oh, my, look at him." A woman nearby gasped to her friend. The pheromones in the room rose, making my nose itch.

"Come home with mama," one of the other women purred.

"Alice, you're married," her friend giggled.

"I'd be anything for him."

I snorted.

"But he's with someone. Poo." the first one pouted. "Think they're together."

"By the way he's about to devour her in front of everyone, I'd say so." She sighed longingly. "Lucky bitch."

"Are you sure you don't want to go back to the room, pet?" Wynn purred, his presence pressing in around the room. "We could share a bottle back there."

Piper's lovely laughter filled my ears. "No, behave. You said you'd take me out. I don't want to go back to the room just yet. I practically live there now." A bit of bitterness leaked out of her voice.

Not that I blamed her. Living in such close quarters wasn't pleasant for either of us. It was probably about time we found somewhere more permanent to settle. Especially since Antoine had implied, it would be a while.

"Oh, there's Darren," Piper whispered, forgetting I could hear her just as easily as if she were right next to me. "Should we go say hello?"

Wynn chuckled. "He can hear you, love. Besides, let the man have his drink alone. There's a booth over there."

Piper hummed. "Alright, I guess you're right."

My eyes lifted to the mirror behind the bar. I tracked them as they walked behind me and over to a booth on the opposite side of the room. Piper wore the dress she bought but hadn't worn since we arrived. It clung to her form nicely, enveloping her body like it was meant for it. Her heels accentuated her legs and made her already perfect ass even better.

Wynn's hand slid down her mostly bare back and cupped her backside, giving me a smirk over his shoulder.

I didn't react, drinking from my tumbler as if I weren't bothered by his blatant attempt to rub her in my face.

Piper smacked his hand away, making me smirk.

"Here you go, honey." Trixie sat the wings in front of me and hovered for longer than needed. "Can I get you something else?"

A glance in the mirror told me Piper was listening. Her eyes darted in my direction every so often as if she were trying not to look.

I offered her a dazzling smile. "You get off at two, was it?"

Chapter 9

Piper

THE CLACKING OF THE keyboard was hard to get used to. I hadn't been in a work environment like here at Biggs Law Firm in a long while.

At first, the silence and clacking were annoying. When I worked as a maid, at least, I had Darren and Gretchen to talk to most days. Then the Durands popped up randomly. If the day was too quiet, I could always pop in my earbuds as I worked.

Here, I had Bethany. Mr. Biggs' red-headed paralegal.

"Hey, fax these over to the courthouse, will ya?" Bethany rolled over in her desk chair, her curly red hair bouncing around her shoulders. Then she slapped the papers on my desk with a smile.

"Sure, no problem." I took the papers and smiled in return. I turned my attention back to the computer, but Bethany didn't leave. She leaned her elbows on the edge of my desk, her face in her hands as she watched me. She watched me the way people did to zoo animals, with mild curiosity and a bit of boredom.

"Yes?" I drew out, arching a brow.

Bethany cocked her head to the side, staring at me intently. "What's your story?"

I sighed and turned back to my computer. "I told you. I got dumped here for work, and then that company went under. I liked it here, so I stayed."

Snorting, Bethany lifted her head off her hands. "Yeah, okay. But you've been here for a month now, and I don't know anything about you except that. Not where you're from. Anything about your family." She gave me a sly grin, wagging her brows. "If you have a boyfriend."

I smiled to myself.

"Or maybe a girlfriend."

"No, no girlfriend." I looked at her briefly. She wasn't going to let this go. Turning from the computer, I huffed. "How about this? After work, we can go down to The Croaking Parrot, get a drink, and I'll tell you all about little old Piper Billings. Okay?"

"Yes!" Bethany grinned triumphantly, smacking her hands on the top of my desk.

I flinched as the pens rattled in their holder, threatening to fall over.

"I'm going to hold you to that," Bethany pointed at me as she rolled backward away from my desk and back over to hers where the incessant clacking began again.

Sighing once more, I picked up the papers Bethany wanted me to fax and stood. The office at Biggs Law Firm was spacious but small. If that made sense. It was big enough to house my desk at the front of the office, where I played the guard to all those who wished to see Mr. Biggs. A row of chairs and an overly squishy couch worked as our waiting area where I kept it stocked with out of date magazines and that day's paper.

Bethany's desk took up the other half of the central area. I tried to stay away from her desk which was more of a mess than Drake's bedroom. It was distracting to my maidly ways, but it would be hard to explain why I had such a cleaning fix. So, I stayed away.

The only fax machine in the whole building sat at the end of my reception area. Meaning, they all gave their faxes to me. It was part of my job, but still having them coming in and out of my space, just dumping whatever on my desk was kind of annoying.

Mr. Biggs himself had a large office in the back of the building with a door he kept shut the majority of the time. Occasionally, he'd come out to tell me something he needed done - files put away, papers faxed, or changes to his schedule. He was nice enough but worked a lot. I haven't seen him leave the office before Bethany and myself once.

Bethany talked more to me than Mr. Biggs did. I half thought he didn't like me, but Bethany had reassured me that was just his personality. Mr. Biggs could be charming when he wanted to be, but when he was working, he could be short-sighted.

The hours went by, and the clock ticked down to closing time. I felt each one of those minutes knowing I had to figure something out to tell Bethany to get her off my back. I couldn't tell her the truth, and lying to her would only complicate things.

"Piper," the front door opened, and the mailman came in with an armful of packages. "Got a big one for you today."

"Oh, yeah?" I grinned at Tony, a short, pudgy fifty-year-old man who flirted like he breathed. He was harmless and never pushed beyond a slight compliment here or an innuendo there. "I hope it won't give me any trouble."

Tony placed the package on my desk. "Oh, I think you can handle it."

I rolled my eyes, looking at the box. "Just like a man, promising a big night and only delivering an average size outcome."

Chuckling, Tony offered me his device to sign. "What can I say? I choose to be optimistic."

"Yeah, yeah. Keep dreaming." I signed the screen and handed it back, before picking up the envelopes next to the box. "Thanks, Tony," I said while sorting out the mail.

Tony left, and I walked over to Bethany's desk with her mail.

She was on the phone.

"I don't care if you have to stay up all night. Find me those depositions!" Bethany smiled at me and mouthed thank you as I placed her mail on her desk.

Spinning on my heel, my feet ate up the small distance between Bethany's office and Mr. Biggs. I went to put his mail in the box by his door. Before I could slide the envelopes home, the door opened.

"Oh, Piper. Just the person I was looking for." Mr. Biggs's warm brown eyes smiled down at me. His black hair gleamed in the light, making it almost blue in color. A dimple peeked out on one side of his face that would make any other woman fawn over him.

I was neck-deep in sexy vampires and thus immune to his charms.

"Mr. Biggs, I was just bringing you your mail." I handed him the stack of envelopes with a polite nod.

Mr. Biggs' hand wrapped around the envelopes, his fingers brushing mine purposely. "You can call me Jack. I think you've been here long enough to drop the formalities."

Uncomfortable with his familiarity, I chewed on the inside of my cheek and nodded once. "Did you need anything else?"

Mr. Biggs stared down at me for a moment longer than was normal before shaking his head. "You are an enigma, Piper. What did we do to deserve someone like you?"

I shifted in place awkwardly. "I don't know about all that. I have hardly done anything worth the praise. Just doing my job."

Bethany giggled from her desk. "Which in and of itself is a miracle. You wouldn't believe how many incompetent receptionists we have had. Most can't even work the email system, let alone answer phones like a normal human being."

I shrugged. "I'm just glad I can help."

Mr. Biggs placed his hand on my shoulder and gave me a small squeeze. "We appreciate it more than we can say."

A tight smile was my only reply. Either Mr. Biggs was this friendly with all his coworkers - something I had yet to see with Bethany - or he was interested in me. I hoped for the former, but I didn't have that kind of luck.

Thankfully, the phone rang.

I thumbed back towards my desk. "I better get that."

Without waiting for an answer, I hurried back to my space. Grabbing the phone off the receiver, I put it to my ear at the same time I shifted the box on the counter over to me. "Biggs Law Firm, how may I help you?"

The box didn't have a return name, only an address. One I didn't recognize.

"Have you received my gift yet?" A smooth, seductive voice oozed into my ears and made me shimmy in place.

My eyes widened. Glancing around the office hurriedly, I held the phone closer to my face as I whispered fiercely, "Wynn?"

"Why, my lovely, have you forgotten me already?" His voice was low and sultry, a caress along my skin with each word.

I resisted the urge to roll my eyes and grabbed the box cutter out of my drawer. "You know I haven't. What did you send me?"

"So, you did receive it." The smile in his voice did strange things to my insides. "And you haven't opened it yet. I so wished it so."

I sighed and cautiously cut the box open, keeping my voice low. "I swear if this is another skirt, I already told you, I bought a new one. You don't need to keep buying me things. I have a job."

"Yes," Wynn's voice sobered. "You do. And you should not forget it while playing assistant to the charming lawyer."

I paused for a moment, mid-opening of the box, and stared at the phone. "Wynn...are you jealous?"

The phone was silent for a long time before Wynn finally answered. "Perhaps. Is that so strange?"

I couldn't help the silly smile that crept up my face as I pulled the edges of the box open and delved through the tissue paper. A small piece of paper read, "Made custom with you in mind."

My brows drew down as I reached further into the box and wrapped my hands around a soft yet rubbery item. Not lifting it from its container, my fingers felt along the long expansion of what I was beginning to suspect was not safe for work. Evenly spaced ridges decorated the sides of it until I reached the end where it flared out into a circular dipped surface.

Swallowing thickly, I glanced back where Mr. Biggs's door was firmly closed once more, and Bethany was on the phone again.

Turning back to the phone, my hand still inside the box, I hissed, "Wynn Durand, did you send me a dildo? To my work?" I had a hard time keeping my voice low. My face was on fire, and I tried my best to keep it hidden from Bethany.

"Do you not like it?" Wynn pouted quietly. "I made a mold of my own for you. The website said it would help us with the distance between us."

Wynn had been trying. He really had been. Ever since I brought up the fact that I felt more like his whore than his girlfriend, he'd sent me flowers, chocolates, and all kinds of other gifts. It must have gotten out because Rayne and the twins had also begun to send me things as well. Though nothing like this.

The only one who had yet to send me a gift was Antoine. I supposed the head of the Durand house thought he was too good to woo me. Not that I needed gifts, but it was nice to be appreciated. Wanted. Especially with the distance and limited ability to speak to one another.

"It's great, Wynn. Really. But next time, send it to my hotel, not where I work," I tried my best to keep my voice even and not chastising.

"You ready to go?" Bethany appeared at my side, making me jump.

I hastily closed the box and muttered into the phone. "I gotta go, bye."

Turning to Bethany, I grimaced. "Actually, I'm going to have to take a rain check. I'm sorry."

Bethany's lower lip pushed out in a pout. "Oh, poop. Alright. I guess it can't be helped." She pointed a finger at me, her eyes narrowed. "But, I'm going to get you to spill the beans one of these days, girl."

I smiled tightly. "Of course."

When hell freezes over.

Chapter 10

Darren

IT WAS THAT TIME of the month again. No, not the time that made Piper unbearable to live with. The time in which one member of the House of Durand would show up for the day or rather night. It was all they could give us, and I would be lying if I didn't look forward to it.

Things between Piper and myself had been strained since Master Wynn left. It didn't help that the vampire had bombarded the hotel room with gifts nonstop since he left. I suppose Master Wynn was trying to make up for something. Unfortunately, the other masters had taken to the idea as well. I hoped all the groveling would end soon. We were running out of room for such things.

Piper would be home any moment now.

It was strange to have the whole room to myself while she went to her new day job. Quiet. Too quiet. I could admit that I missed her incessant chattering—the moment to moment sounds that came from my coworker and roommate. Even after a month of being alone, I still couldn't get used to it.

The silence was probably what did me in. It was why I spent more time out getting coffee that I didn't want and food I didn't need. It was on my way home from such a trip that I noticed Piper stalking toward the hotel room door like the devil himself was on her heels.

Her eyes darted around her suspiciously, and her hands clasped around a brown box pressed tightly against her chest. Frowning, I walked a little faster until I was entering the room just after Piper.

Piper jumped at my entry. She shoved something flesh-colored back into the box on the bed and spun around, her face redder than a tomato.

"Uh, Darren. Hey. What's up? Any sign of our lord and masters?" She chuckled nervously, her fingers fidgeting in front of her as she tried to play off her nerves with a joke.

Pursing my lips, I stepped toward her. "What is it you have there?"

Piper half turned before she caught herself. "What? This? Oh, nothing. Just some office supplies." Her giggle came out shaky, and then she hiccupped.

I arched a brow.

"I do not believe you." I ate up the space between us and reached for the box. "Let me see."

"No!" Piper shouted into my face, grabbing for the box, and clutching it to her chest. "It's nothing. It's personal."

I paused and asked, "I thought you said it was office supplies?"

"It is." Piper quickly answered and then added on, "It's my own personal office supplies. Now hands off."

"Very well," I stepped away from her as she sighed and lowered her arms, letting her guard down. Without warning, I reached around her and snatched the box from her hand.

"Darren!" she screeched, trying to climb on my back and take the box from me as I turned away from her. "Give it back right now."

Shifting around to keep her away from the box, I popped it opened and withdrew...my brows furrowed...a dildo?

"Jesus fuck, Darren!" She jumped over my shoulder and grabbed the offending item, then shoved it back into the box with a huff. Piper blew her hair out of her face with a scowl. "Next time I say it is personal, I mean it's personal. Jeez."

"My apologies," I stuttered out when the shock finally passed. My face warmed. I hurried by Piper and over to my desk, where I promptly sat down and busied myself with the household accounts.

Piper shuffled around the room, no doubt hiding her new...item.

A part of me was appalled that I had even considered insisting on seeing what she had even after she claimed it was personal. Her red face had been enough to tip me off to what I would find. And yet another part of me needed to know what it was that made her so flustered.

Now that I knew what was in the box, all I could think about was Piper using it. The numbers on the computer in front of me blurred together. Instead of seeing spreadsheets, all I saw was Piper spreading her legs, working herself up so the long length of the toy would slide right into her needy folds.

I swallowed thickly and shook my head, forcing myself to push the image from my mind.

"Darren..." Piper's voice came from behind me quiet and unsure. "Uh, could we talk?"

I shifted around in my chair, my gaze landing on her forehead instead of her eyes. Damn it all. Why was I so bothered by a toy? It wasn't like I haven't seen one before. Antoine and I had used several just like the one in Piper's box. It wasn't anything new.

But it was Piper's. Not mine. Not Antoine's. Piper's.

"Yes?" I internally patted myself on the back for not sounding as shaken as I felt.

Piper sat on the edge of her bed just across from me, her hands in her lap and her eyes looking anywhere but me. "Uh, I was wondering if you knew who was coming today?" She brushed a strand of hair behind her ear and shifted on the bed. "I mean, did anyone say -"

"No."

"Oh, okay." Piper nodded, seemingly working herself up to say something else but not following through. She stood and turned away, moving to the dresser. She opened a drawer and began to pull out clothing.

I twisted back around to the computer.

"I'm going to change. What do you want for dinner?" Piper continued talking as if we hadn't just had an embarrassing experience. "I don't know about you, but I could do with something leafy today. I'm getting a bit tired of fried food." She groaned and touched her stomach. "I need to find a gym or something, or I'm going to end up as big as a house. I never thought I'd say I missed cleaning that huge place." Piper turned her head to me, grinning so brightly her eyes squinted tight.

I nodded. "I know what you mean."

Piper crossed the room behind me and entered the bathroom. The door closed, and I sagged slightly happy not to face her for a moment.

"Should we wait and see if someone shows up?" Piper asked through the bathroom door. "I don't know if my stomach can wait until full dark."

I snorted. No, I doubted she could. When it came between Piper and food, always just give it to her. You'll save yourself a lot of pain, physically and emotionally.

"Who do you think is coming this time?" Piper opened the door appearing in a pair of shorts and a t-shirt. "I hope it's not the twins. I love them, but they are too much to handle all at once in such a short time, you know?"

I inclined my head and stood from the desk.

I did, indeed know. I'd been with the family for far longer than I had been a regular human. I knew all the ups and downs of every member of the House of Durand. The twins were quite a lot to handle on any given day, let alone when they were trying to provide her with all their love and affection in one twenty-four-hour time frame.

"Anyway," Piper continued heading for the door where she shoved on her flip flops. "I'd take the twins over Antoine any day." Piper chuckled and wrinkled her nose. "His domineering ways are okay in the bedroom, but I just can't deal with him today."

A part of me didn't want Antoine to be the one this time either. While I longed to see the master vampire, I feared what he would do to the budding feelings that were spreading inside of me.

I opened the door for Piper, my gaze locked on her face as if seeing her for the first time. What was it about her that had changed for me? We haven't had another moment in a few weeks, and I thought I was over it. That she was over it. I was only kidding myself. That strange attraction to her had only been waiting beneath the surface, waiting to rear its ugly head. Now it had, and I didn't know what to do.

Waiting for Piper to exit first, she moved to the door but didn't exit. Her happy expression morphed into one of horror as she froze in place. Piper gave a sheepish smile as she wiggled her fingers in greeting. "Oh, hi, Antoine."

Chapter 11
Piper

"WHAT A PLEASANT COINCIDENCE." Antoine laced his fingers in front of him, his eyes shifting between Darren and me. "Are we heading to dinner?" His lips tipped up, his fang flashing briefly, making his words more menacing than they implied.

I grinned mischievously, eyeballing Darren from the corner of my eye. "Oh, yeah. We were just going to Frankie's." I pushed past him and said over my shoulder, "You like corn dogs, right?"

Darren made a choking sound behind me, but I continued to strut down the sidewalk. Did I care that I basically talked shit about a master vampire within hearing distance? Not really. Okay, a little. But only so much in the fact that Antoine could be scary when met head on. Pretending I'd done nothing wrong was the only way to get away with...well...anything.

"Master, we were not expecting you until later." Darren, always the suck-up, trailed behind with the 'master.'

Gag me with a spoon. I didn't know how Darren did it. I barely gave Antoine the respect an employer required. Let alone kiss ass the way he did, and I was boinking the vampire too. Not as much as Darren. Maybe it required centuries of sucking dick to finally make it to the ass-kissing.

I giggled to myself.

"What pray tell has caused your amusement?" Antoine appeared at my side, his pale eyes watching my face.

Clucking my tongue, I lifted my chin up a bit and laced my fingers behind my back. "Nothing. Can't I be happy to see you?"

Antoine scoffed. "Hardly. You cannot pretend to be excited to see me after blatantly expressing your reluctance so adamantly before."

I turned on my heel, so I was walking backward, smiling innocently up at him. "Did I?"

Those icy blue eyes narrowed on me. "Do you really wish to spend the precious time we have playing games?"

Sauntering up to Antoine, Darren standing off to one side with a disapproving frown, I reached for Antoine's expensive maroon tie. Everything Antoine wore cost more than I made in a week, and the Durands paid me quite well. Antoine allowed me to paw at him, not even bothered by me crinkling the silk.

I stroked my fingers up and down his tie, making sure my body pressed just barely against the line of Antoine's. Peering up at him beneath my lashes, I licked my lips and murmured, "I thought you liked to play games? Or do you only save those for Darren?" My gaze slid to the side where Darren stiffened.

Long fingers wrapped around my hand firmly. They didn't push me away but pulled me closer. Antoine's silvery-white hair fell over his shoulders as he leaned down to me, his lips against the side of my head. "If it is games you seek, let us retire to the room and I will give you your every desire."

A shudder ran down my body and settled low between my thighs as if Antoine had touched me physically. My lips parted in a gasp. I should have known better than to play with Antoine. Not only could he feel what I was feeling, but he was better at it. I supposed centuries of practice would do that to you.

Licking my lips once more, I trailed my fingers through the length of his hair and brushed my cheek against his own until my mouth was on the shell of his ear. "Not until you feed me."

Pushing away from Antoine with a laugh, I wasn't prepared for the hand that grabbed the back of my neck and jerked me back around. My eyes widened. Antoine's lips crashed onto mine, his hand on the base of my neck, keeping me from moving in any way he didn't want me to.

The sharp edges of Antoine's fangs pressed against my lips, giving me the option to either open my mouth to him or get cut.

While I despised being manhandled, I had provoked him on purpose. What did I expect to happen?

Opening my mouth to him, I lightly traced my tongue along the line of his fangs, being careful not to nick myself. French kissing vampires was a tricky business. If you got too out of control, you'd end up with a tongue piercing.

Not pleasant.

My hands slid up the lapels of Antoine's suit jacket and curled into the hair at the nape of his neck, pulling him closer to me. Manhandled or not, I wasn't about to let him be in complete control. The fingers on the back of my neck loosened, allowing me more control of my head.

I briefly wondered what we looked like, standing in front of the hotel, making out like teenagers. Antoine's eyes were closed, but instead of shutting mine as well, I moved my eyes to the side, searching for Darren.

The butler stood to the side of us, just out of arm's reach. Usually, Darren's gaze was anywhere but on me and whatever Durand was trying to get into my pants that day. Not so today. Those dark orbs watched Antoine and I like a man starved. Desire and jealousy flared in his face. I wasn't sure if it was for Antoine or for me. Maybe both?

No, it couldn't be.

Then I remembered what I'd heard a few weeks ago in full clarity. Darren wanted me. He also wanted Antoine. Watching us kiss must be killing him right now. I didn't know why, but I didn't like it. It made my stomach all squishy.

Antoine pulled away. His swollen lips frowning. "What is it?"

I pulled my gaze back to Antoine and forced a smile. "Nothing. Let's go eat. I'm starving."

For a moment, Antoine looked like he was going to argue but then nodded.

I slid my hand into Antoine's.

The master vampire's brows rose, but he didn't remove it.

Holding a hand out to Darren, I smiled brightly. "Coming?"

Chapter 12

Darren

PRIVATE TIME WAS NONEXISTENT in the hotel room. There was no way for either Piper or me to be alone with Antoine without asking the other to leave. They had not asked me to leave.

As amusing as it was to watch Piper bully Antoine into eating a corn dog, I hadn't been able to eat a bite. My body ached. It ached in a way that could only come from going too long without being touched by another human being.

The bartender, Trixie's number was still on my desk, but I'd never use it. It wasn't just loyalty to Antoine that kept me from using her body to quell my loneliness. I had my lovers over the years. None of them compared to Antoine.

Except it wasn't just Antoine, I wanted.

Antoine was safety, comfort. Like coming home after a long trip away. Just having him here with us made it easier to breathe.

But Piper. Piper was something else altogether.

If Antoine was like coming home, then Piper was a tornado ripping through my home causing chaos and maybe a bit of strife. Some might say I resented her ability to disrupt everything she touched. Still, with so much order in my life, the same monotonous day to day, I wanted the chaos. I wanted to touch it. To be a part of it.

The question though was, did Piper want me too?

The way she had looked at me while kissing Antoine made me hope. And hope was a dangerous thing.

"Want a drink?" Piper asked Antoine, kneeling by the mini-fridge. She grabbed a tiny bottle of scotch and tossed it at me without asking if I wanted it. She removed a small bottle of white wine for herself.

Antoine's eyes darkened with hunger, his gaze sweeping over her crouched form. "Yes, I would."

Piper swallowed audibly and then let out a nervous giggle. "This hotel might be good, but I don't think they have what you're wanting." She stood, and her gaze flickered to me once before she swayed her way over to the chair Antoine sat on by the door.

Giving me her back, Piper slid one leg on either side of Antoine, her short shorts stretching tightly across her backside. I didn't know if the view was on purpose or not. Then Piper tossed her blonde hair over her shoulder and smirked my way.

I twisted the top off the scotch and downed the whole thing in one go.

Piper's words were low as a whisper as if she were nervous to say it, "I have an idea."

Antoine placed his hands on her hips, allowing her to settle onto his lap. "Oh? And what pray tell does the great Piper demand of her master today?"

A snort escaped before I could stop it. The thought of anyone being the master of the woman who had disrupted our lives so much was laughable. Not even Antoine could claim to be such and pretending to be so would only needle her into a frenzy.

"I'm going to pretend you didn't say that." Piper's volume lifted slightly.

"You may pretend whatever you like, but it does not stop it from being true." Antoine stroked his fingers under the line of her shirt, and her body rippled against his touch.

"Do you want to hear my idea or not?" Piper huffed, placing her hands over Antoine's, stopping their trek up her back.

Antoine laughed. A full-throated one that made my cock stiffen against my trousers. Even with the distance between us, Antoine was still able to affect me so. I wondered if Piper felt the same way.

"Antoine," Piper warned, but her words came out breathy. It seemed our master did affect her as well.

"By all means Piper, tell us your idea." The humor was still there in his voice, but so was something else. Promises of things in the dark. Things I was well acquainted with.

"You want time with both of us...right?" Piper began, shifting herself so she could see me as well. "Instead of making one of us leave so the other can have their time..." she trailed off, her tongue darting out to wet her lips.

My eyes widened.

Was Piper suggesting what I thought she was? No, certainly not. Trying to carefully control my face, I locked eyes with Antoine. How did he feel about this? The last time we three had been in one room together, I had ended up on the wrong side of a riding crop, not that I didn't enjoy it, but still. I did not want to do anything that would upset Antoine. He was possessive and jealous of anyone outside of his brothers. He'd proved that the last time he had tested Piper with me.

Except now...had that changed? The phone call a few weeks ago made me think he was still uncertain about letting me in with both of them or even Piper alone.

"Antoine?" Piper touched his cheek, drawing his attention back to her. "Since we are pressed for time..." she trailed her hand down his face and into the collar of his shirt, playing with his exposed skin before pausing, "what do you think?"

Antoine's pale gaze stayed on me for a moment longer. The only emotion I read in his gaze was suspicion. Did he think I had something to do with this? I dropped my eyes to the bed.

"Is this what you want, Piper?" Antoine asked, his voice carefully neutral. "To be with us both at the same time?"

Piper sucked in a breath, making my eyes lift slightly to see her face redden. "I was thinking more along the lines of something else..."

"Then, please elaborate," Antoine commanded, just a hint of his power pushing into the room. "Let there be no confusion between us."

I waited with bated breath for Piper to explain what she meant, but she didn't. Piper smacked Antoine on the chest and shifted to move out of his lap, his grip on her thighs instantly stopped her. "No," Piper wiggled in his lap, her voice hard. "If you're going to be a dick, forget it. You can just spend your time with Darren. I'll go find a movie to watch or something."

Antoine sighed, all the tension leaving his body. "My apologies. I did not mean to lose control like that. It has been a trying time."

Piper stopped trying to get away and stared down at him. "You know how much I hate when you use your powers on me without permission."

"I am aware. I apologize once more." Antoine dipped his head.

"If you know, then you shouldn't do it."

Why Antoine hadn't beat her ass red at her insolence was beyond me. She wasn't even talking back to me, and I wanted to spank her for being such a pain in the ass.

"Time passes quickly while we debate, Piper," Antoine reminded Piper pointedly. Piper didn't say anything, and he added, "Please."

Piper seemed to accept the plea because she relaxed. "Have you ever bitten someone while..." she paused and ducked her head, shy all of a sudden.

Antoine's lips curved up at the edges. "While inside of someone else? Why Piper...where could you have gotten such a naughty thought from?" Those icy orbs slid over to me.

I didn't bother to defend myself against the accusation in his eyes.

"It wasn't Darren's idea, so don't get mad at him." Piper snapped her fingers in front of Antoine's face. The only person who would ever get away with such an action alive or undead.

"Then let us put your new fantasy into reality before the sun takes away our time together." He lifted Piper up and out of the chair, bringing her over to the bed. Antoine sat her down beside me, not even causing the mattress to shift.

"Wait, wait." Piper held her hands up and turned to me. "You didn't even ask if Darren was okay with it?" Her cheeks were red as she said it, unable to meet my eyes.

Antoine glanced down at her and then over to me. "Well? What say you, Darren?"

I didn't need to think about it. The thought of being pressed against Piper's sweet body while Antoine fucked her and bit me was too much like a dream. My answer came out a scratchy stutter, "Yes. Yes. Please."

Chapter 13

Piper

WHAT THE HELL HAD I been thinking? Had I really suggested we have a threesome? Because make no mistake, that was what it would have been. Biting could be just as pleasurable as sex for both human and vampire.

I didn't know what had come over me. What had made me think of it. Wait. I did know.

Darren.

One look at Darren when I was in Antoine's arms, and a fist clenched around my heart. The want in his gaze. The pure need. It pulled something low inside of me, and I knew I couldn't do it. I couldn't ask him to leave so Antoine and I could have alone time.

Hence my not so brilliant idea.

"Piper," Antoine touched the side of my face bringing my eyes back to him. "Are you sure this is what you want?"

No. Yes. Fuck if I knew. But I couldn't make Darren leave.

To Antoine, I nodded tightly, not trusting my voice.

"Very well." Antoine lifted me up in his arms, his hands beneath my thighs. To say he walked would have been wrong. We floated over to the bed where he laid me down between himself and Darren. Not touching the other, but near him.

Antoine lay pressed up against my back, his fingers caressing down my arm but not pushing me to go further.

Was he waiting for me to make the first move?

I blinked up at Darren, at a loss for what I was supposed to do next. I'd suggested it but hell if I knew how to go about it. The twins had been my first threesome. Plus, no one had sunk fangs into anyone then.

Something must have shown on my face because Darren moved to leave.

I reached out and grabbed his wrist saying, "Don't. Don't go."

Darren gave me a sad smile. "Do not force yourself to do something you do not want."

That pissed me off.

Jerking him by the wrist, I pulled him back onto the bed. When he was within reach, I grabbed the front of his pristine button-down shirt, wrinkling it in my grasp. The expression on Darren's face at the action was a mixture of horror and surprise. When I pressed my mouth to his, a small sound escaped his throat. I swallowed the sound as my tongue darted across his lips. Antoine's hand tightened on my waist, but I didn't stop.

Tentatively, Darren touched the side of my face as if afraid I'd break. His mouth opened beneath me, and for the first time, our tongues touched.

Just like anything else in his life, Darren was thorough. His tongue swept over mine, touching and tasting every inch of it before sliding along my teeth and inside of my cheeks. The hand on my face moved to the back of my neck, angling me slightly to the side as he pressed his body closer to me.

With Antoine at my back, the hardness of his cock against my butt and Darren at my front, I was feeling a bit overwhelmed. I pulled back from the kiss breathing heavily, my cheeks burning at what I'd just done.

I mustered up as much attitude as I could and scowled, "Don't tell me what I want."

Antoine laughed. The feeling of it reverberated along my back and sank low into places it should not have been able to touch. Darren stiffened at the sound, wary of his master...our master.

"I do not know why I feared the two of you embracing." I turned my head to see the amusement on Antoine's face. "You would be just as much his master as I am yours."

I arched a brow. "You aren't my master."

Antoine flashed a fanged grin. "*Exactament.*"

Not understanding what Antoine was talking about, I shifted the topic. "So, how do we do this?" I began to pull my shirt overhead. "I might have suggested it, but the logistics are lost on me."

Darren smirked, his eyes watching my every movement, cautiously flickering to Antoine every once in a while. He feared Antoine's reaction but not enough to stop staring at the skin I exposed.

Antoine placed a possessive arm around my shoulders, drawing me to him. His mouth hovered over the pulse of my neck while he unsnapped my bra. My breasts hung heavy, the skin prickling, and my nipples tightening at Darren's hot gaze.

I opened my mouth to tell Antoine to stop teasing him, but he beat me to it.

"Disrobe." The commanding power in Antoine's voice was hard to ignore, but it wasn't for me.

Darren stood. His fingers went to the buttons of his shirt, undoing them one by one. My gaze ate up each inch of skin he revealed, licking my lips. He shrugged out of his jacket and shirt and I watched them fall to the floor with more fascination than I'd had for anything else.

My eyes move back to Darren's naked chest. He wasn't built like the twins, or slender like Wynn and Rayne. His shoulders were broad, and the muscle on his chest made me wonder how he hid all of it beneath his suits. Good tailors, I supposed. My hands itched to touch the ridges along his stomach, to trail the dark hair that made a path into his pants.

When Darren's hands went to the waist of his pants, my breath caught. The snap of the button and unzipping reverberated in the quiet of the room.

"Touch him, Piper," Antoine's voice murmured in my ear, his fingers dragging down the side of my shorts before teasing the edge of my pubic bone. "I can feel your heart race with need. Touch our Darren. I know you want to."

Licking my lips, I lifted my eyes to meet Darren's. He had paused in his movements at Antoine's words, waiting to see what I would do.

I slid away from Antoine, my arm going out the few feet between us to touch Darren's stomach. My fingertips trailed over the muscles, marveling at the strength beneath the smooth skin. I was having a hard time imagining Darren at the gym. He didn't seem the type to work on his body the way he worked on the carpets at the manor. It made me wonder what else I didn't know about Darren.

When I found the edge of his underwear peeking out from his undone pants, Darren sucked in a breath.

I hesitated.

"Help him," Antoine encouraged in my ear, his fingers playing along my hip bone. "Touch him as I touch you."

I sat up slightly so I could use my other hand and grabbed both sides of Darren's pants. My gaze lifted to Darren's, watching him as I dragged the pants down off his hips. He wore dark blue boxer briefs that clung to his hips and thick thighs. I laughed slightly.

"Something funny?" Darren asked his voice rough and low.

I smiled up at him. "I don't know why, but I expected whitey tighties."

Darren's lips jerked.

Antoine's fingers dipped beneath the waistband of my shorts, bringing my attention back to the task at hand.

I had a brief moment where I couldn't do anything but breathe, and even that came out as a stuttering moan. I pushed at

Antoine's hand. "I can't concentrate when you do that."

His laughter rumbled against my back. "My apologies." Shifting his hand back to my hip, he urged me on, "Finish it, Piper."

Moving out of Antoine's embrace, I pushed up to my knees, so I sat before Darren on the edge of the bed. Breathing deeply, I reached for the last article of clothing. I held my breath as I pulled the elastic down his hips, exposing the top of his pubic hair. I shifted closer on my knees, reaching behind Darren to slide the fabric over his buttocks.

My finger skimmed the skin of his butt, and I somehow remembered how to breathe. Then I realized how very close I had brought myself to Darren. Staring intensely into his dark gaze, I pushed his underwear the final length letting it fall down his legs.

I wanted to look. I wanted to look so badly it hurt. Except for a part of me knew that if I did, something would change between us. I'd seen his dick before in the office with Antoine.

At that time though, I'd been pissed off and not in the mood to play. I wanted to play now.

Darren was incredibly careful not to touch me. Almost as if he were afraid. I glanced back at Antoine, making sure he hadn't suddenly changed his mind as he was prone to do.

The heat in Antoine's eyes sent a shiver of need through me. No. He hadn't changed his mind.

Turning back to Darren, I let my eyes drop. There was a spackle of dark hair around his length. Neatly trimmed as expected. Not surprisingly, Darren wasn't circumcised. The only one of the men cut besides Marcus, I didn't know what was going on in his pants, was Rayne. Which made sense. Rayne was the youngest of them and didn't become a vampire until circumcision was popular with humans.

"What is it?" Darren breathed out heavily.

I shook my head. "Nothing."

Antoine's hand picked up mine, his bare body pressed against my back. When he'd moved or even when he'd disrobed, I didn't know.

I allowed Antoine to lead my hand toward Darren. Somehow, wrapping my hand around the hot length of Darren with Antoine was sexier than if I'd done it myself. The small sound Darren let out as Antoine stroked my hand down him made me smile.

We worked Darren until he was panting. He reached a hand out and grabbed Antoine's shoulder behind me, bracing himself.

Antoine released my hand and pulled my shorts and panties down in one movement. I was left holding Darren's cock in my hands while Antoine bent me slightly, the head of his own length rubbing against my slit.

I was already wet and ready for him after all the build-up from touching Darren. Antoine slid into me in one go, my shorts keeping me from spreading my legs further, making the fit tighter than usual.

Gasping, my hand stopped moving up and down Darren, instead just holding him there between us, one hand on his waist to steady myself.

Antoine thrust into me, not giving me a momentary reprieve. He grunted to Darren a moment later, "Touch her, Darren. As you always wished."

I glanced up at Darren, curious at what he wanted to do. What he would do.

Those gloved hands lifted - because even naked, he never removed the gloves - and reached out to touch me. I pulled back from him, causing him to frown, and a flash of hurt crossed his face before he built that blank wall back up.

Shaking my head at him, I gasped out, "Gloves. Take. Off." Antoine hadn't stopped, making it harder to get what I wanted across.

Understanding and relief crossed Darren's face. Biting the finger of one glove, Darren slowly pulled it off. I watched with growing fascination as it dropped to the bed between us. Then the other one. Neither of us went to move them.

Those hands were the only part of him that was rougher than the rest. They cupped my breasts, holding the weight of them in his hands before flicking the tips with the rough pad of his thumb.

I gasped and arched into his touch, my eyes fluttering shut.

Antoine's mouth moved to my ear, his thrusts slowing, "Take him in your mouth, Piper."

I jerked, my eyes snapping open. Darren's expression was carefully neutral.

My hand wrapped around his length once more, finding it harder than ever and twitching slightly in my grasp. Keeping my eyes on Darren, I leaned forward and pressed my mouth to his chin. Then I kissed his collar bone, dragging my mouth down his chest, only stopping briefly to lick his nipple. Darren flinched in my hand, making me smile.

I licked a path down his delicious abs until my mouth met my hand. I kissed the tip of him, lapping at the liquid coming out. Darren hissed. His hands sitting on the back of my head but not pushing.

Darren and Antoine leaned forward, draping me in shadow. I slid my mouth over the head of Darren, sucking him down until I couldn't go any further. I knew the moment that Antoine bit Darren. The hands on the back of my head tightened in my hair, and his hips jerked forward, shoving him further down my throat. I had to force myself to relax so I wouldn't gag and ruin the mood.

I'd never been in this position before, having to focus on two tasks at once. With the twins, they had done most of the work. I had just had to hang on for the ride. With Darren in both of our mouths, Antoine had picked up his pace once more, and I could hardly focus on staying upright, let alone sucking. Darren, thankfully, didn't seem to mind though.

The sharp tinge of copper mixed with sex filled the air, and I didn't find it disdainful. If anything, it made my inside tighten around Antoine and my hips to buck harder.

"Master," Darren panted, his muscles tightening by my hand on his hips.

Antoine's answer to Darren's plea was to reach between us, flicking his finger expertly across my clit. That one single swipe sent me over the edge.

I cried out against Darren's cock, and the world exploded behind my eyes. Darren pulled out and spilled himself all over my chest shortly after my release. The hot feel of his seed on my skin made my body quake, and I felt myself moving toward another crest.

Antoine released Darren, letting the blood dribble down the man's chest and drip onto me. I wanted to be disgusted. I should have been. Bodily fluids from sex were one thing, but blood?

I blamed the blood bond with Antoine because all the blood did was make me moan.

Darren collapsed against the side of the bed, spent.

Antoine wasn't done with me yet. Pulling out of me, I found myself on my back with Antoine cleaning the blood and semen off my skin.

When he buried his face between my thighs, I screamed. I couldn't take it anymore. I was going to pass out if I came again. I just knew it.

And yet, I grabbed a handful of Antoine's pale locks and held him close to me, urging him with whimpers and moans. I caught sight of Darren at the edge of the bed, his head lulling to the side as if in a drugged state, watching me with desire in his eyes. It was that look that had made me fall again. It was his dark eyes I saw as everything faded into nothing.

Chapter 14

Darren

A CROW WAS SITTING in the parking lot of the hotel. It had been there almost every single day since Antoine had left.

I wasn't sure if I should be fearful or flattered by Antoine's animal watching us. Watching me. I almost wondered if Antoine was worried...about me? Out of all the years Antoine and I had been together, never did I think he would ever be concerned about losing a woman or a man to me.

Jealousy, I understood. The way the crow kept a watchful eye on us, I did not understand.

I closed the curtains of the hotel room and went to the door. Piper had passed out after our encounter with Antoine, leaving the two of us alone. At that time, naked and satisfied, I never thought about what would happen afterward.

Antoine did.

"She is not yours," he told me, staring at the wall. "No matter what this makes you feel, she does not belong to you alone. Do not let the illusion of domestic bliss fool you."

I had simply nodded my head, not arguing, or believing Piper would ever pick me over the Durands. They were all strong and beautiful in their own right. Everything I was, came from Antoine. I had been nothing, and he made me everything. Made me belong. Made my life mean something. The very thought that Piper - or anyone - would ever pick me over them was laughable. Unthinkable.

And yet...Antoine feared it.

It was a useless fear. There was no need to fear Piper choosing me over them. I couldn't even get her in the same room as me other than when we were sleeping now.

If I thought she was avoiding me before, I didn't know what she was doing now. Hiding. That was as close as what I could think to call it. And she was good at it.

Madeline sat at the reception desk. She blinked up at me and grinned. "Why hello there. I feel like I haven't seen you all week."

I nodded. "Work has not been kind to me. Have you seen-"

"Piper?" Madeline cut me off with a bitter smile. "Are you sure you two aren't dating?" When I didn't answer, she pointed a finger toward the door with a sigh. "She left about an hour ago. Didn't say where she was going though."

I inclined my head in thanks.

I always seemed to be chasing after Piper. What did that say about me? Or maybe her? Either way, I found myself searching for her even when I knew where she was. Today though, I'd had about enough of her running. We had to talk.

Once outside in the morning light, I glanced one way and then the other searching for any sign of that blonde head of hair. After a moment, I realized how silly I'd been. Closing my eyes, I breathed in deeply through my nose.

There.

The faint scent of Piper's shampoo. An artificial berry that I'd recognize anywhere as belonging to Piper.

I couldn't always scent for someone. I certainly couldn't do it for a stranger. Piper wasn't a stranger. I'd know her in the dark, even without my ears to hear.

Turning left, I followed the scent with curious intent. Where could she have gone today besides the office? Usually, I'd have found her down by the beach, but the smell passed the exit to the boardwalk and kept going into the business strip.

After a few minutes of walking, the scent grew stronger. Then it brought me to a halt two shops down from where a door opened, and Piper walked out. A sense of relief filled me, followed by apprehension when a large bald man stood just inside the glass door, acting far too familiar with Piper for my liking.

I angled my head and tried to pick up their conversation.

"Tuesdays and Thursdays good for you?"
the man with the low, almost growling voice
asked, raising my shackles even more.

"Yeah," Piper nodded and grinned. "I just
have to figure out something to tell my
roommate."

The man crossed his arms over his
muscular chest and smirked. "So, I'm to be
your dirty little secret, huh?" His tone
implied more than what he meant.

Piper giggled nervously, her body
language shifting in discomfort. "I guess you
could say so. I just don't want him to worry
is all."

"Him, huh? He your boyfriend?"

I found myself leaning more intently to
hear her answer.

Piper hesitated, chewing on her lower lip.
"Uh, no. Nothing like that. I have too many
guys in my life as it is already." She gave
another nervous giggle.

"Well, then I guess I'm already out of the
running before I even had a chance to ask
you out." The man teased with a wink.

"Sorry, Billy," she shrugged and backed
away a bit. "I'm so taken it's not even funny."

The man, Billy, nodded in understanding,
not trying to come on to her further.

"Understandable. I'll see you next Thursday, then. Be sure to wear something comfortable. You'll be sweating your ass off."

"I will. Bye!" She waved and turned toward me, freezing in place. "Darren? What are you doing here?"

My eyes narrowed. I stalked the last few yards over to Piper. "If you would leave a note or message about where you are going, I wouldn't have to keep hunting you down like a dog."

Piper flinched at my tone. "I didn't mean to make you worry, I just didn't..." she paused and grabbed her elbow with her opposite hand as she scuffed her shoe on the ground. "I didn't know how to act."

"Act?" I arched a brow.

"Around you," she answered pointedly.

"Oh," I answered, not sure how to continue. "You still should have left a message. I don't want to have to call the masters to let them know you've been taken or worse..." I trailed off, letting her fill in the blanks. The vampire hunters have been known to do more than kill the human servants in the pursuit of their prey. Vampires, they'd just kill...us, they'd torture for information or hope that our masters would come save us.

Piper placed a hand on my arm. "I will next time. Promise." She offered me a shy smile. "Have you eaten yet?"

I shook my head.

"Great. Cause I could eat a whole pie right about now." Piper grinned and rubbed her stomach.

I found myself smiling back at her. "Then let's do something about that."

Chapter 15

Piper

THIS WAS SUCH A bad idea. I grunted and groaned, limping down the sidewalk after my second class with Billy.

"You did great," Billy called after me. "Be sure to ice your muscles!"

I waved weakly behind me. Billy's laughter followed me, mocking me as I tried my best to keep from crawling on my hands and knees.

Where had I gotten the horrible idea to learn self-defense? Why in the world would I put myself through this kind of torture? I mean, what was I thinking?

Oh, I know what I'd been thinking.

I was tired of waiting. Tired of sitting around while Antoine and the others did God knew what to outrun the vampire hunters. Which didn't seem to be going very well. If it had been, I wouldn't still be stuck here with...Darren.

Sighing, I paused on the sidewalk, finding a bench to collapse on. It wasn't that being here with Darren was horrible. It was the tension and awkwardness between us. I know. I know. It was my fault. I was the one who suggested the threesome. I couldn't very well be upset at him for doing what I wanted to do.

Except I can, and I am.

It wasn't rational. Any therapist would tell me that I was pushing my anger and frustration about the situation onto an easy target. Not that Darren made anything easy, ever.

No, ever since that night with Antoine, I kept seeing Darren differently. Not the same as before. I mean, we've technically had sex with each other before then but not this way. Not purposely trying to bring pleasure to the other.

Now, I couldn't stop noticing things.

The way his hair fell over his face when he was concentrating. How he tugged on his gloves when he was nervous. All the little things that used to be just him, and now they brought a strange fascination that made my pulse race.

Fuck. Yesterday, when Darren passed me the salt, our fingers brushed and I nearly dropped the glass container.

If Darren was affected the same way I was, I couldn't tell. He was the same pain in the ass as before. Overly neat and tidy to the point of OCD. So put together in his appearance, I wanted to push him onto the bed and-

"Ugh!" Why couldn't I get these dirty thoughts about him out of my head?

I gained several strange looks by people passing. I glared at them in return, and then painstakingly stood from the bench.

Limping down the street, I cursed under my breath with each step, "Fuck, shit, fuck, fuck, fuck," until I reached the hotel. I waved weakly at the evening receptionist and tried my best to not look like I was dying, though I felt like I was. Wasn't being a human servant supposed to have all these restorative powers? If so, mine seemed to be broken.

I didn't understand how every single muscle in my body felt like it had gone through ten rounds with a master vampire. Billy wasn't even close to a master vampire. If anything, I was stronger than him, but the fact that I had no idea how to throw a punch, let alone block one, kind of worked against me.

Once at the room, I struggled to get the door unlocked so I leaned my head against the door, and banged it over and over. Suddenly the door wasn't there, and I fell into Darren's waiting arms.

My face pressed against a white T-shirt stretched tight against a warm muscular body. Inhaling deeply, the strong scent of pine needles and something that was purely Darren. When I'd fallen, my hands had automatically wrapped around Darren's waist. My brows furrowed. The material rubbing against my arms weren't that of a pair of dress pants but the rougher texture of blue jeans.

Lifting my head, my mouth falling open as I took him in.

Darren, perfectly put together, never a hair out of place Darren, was wearing jeans and a t-shirt. A quick look at his feet showed tennis shoes—no loafers in sight. I gaped at him for a few more seconds before I realized what I was doing.

Pushing away from him, I flushed deeply. "Uh, thanks."

"Why didn't you just come in?" Darren asked, amusement filling his eyes.

I held my key up. "I couldn't get it to work." I tried to step into the room and winced.

Darren reached for me, his hands still wearing white gloves. "What's wrong?"

Ignoring his question, I pushed past him and frowned at his appearance. "So, you go to all the trouble to change your clothes, but why the gloves?"

Darren looked at his hands briefly, then crossed his arms. "Some things are harder to change than others."

I pursed my lips to one side and arched a brow. "You took them off before when we - uh - you know. And I know you don't wear them in the shower. Why don't you just take them off?"

Cocking his head to one side, Darren asked, "You don't like what I'm wearing? The saleswoman said it was the latest style."

I shook my head and held my hands up. "No. I'm not saying that. You look..." I started and then really looked him over. Damn. The man looked good in anything he wore. I swallowed hard. "You look great. Just the gloves are a bit out of place."

Backing into the room, I couldn't keep the pain off my face. I tripped over something and went down. Darren grabbed me by the arm before I fell on my ass.

"Thanks," I winced and forced a smile. "Again."

"No more changing the subject." Darren held me gently in his arms. "What happened?"

I shook my head and even that hurt. "Don't worry about it. It's self-inflicted." I pushed away from him and hobbled to the bathroom. I could feel Darren like a looming presence over me while I turned the bath on, filling the tub with cold water. I shivered just at the thought of getting into it but knew I'd hurt even more if I didn't do as Billy suggested.

"Piper."

I sat on the toilet set, gritting my teeth the whole way down. "What?" My tone came out snippy, even to me.

Darren stayed in the bathroom doorway, his brows drawn tightly. "Why are you doing this to yourself?"

Giving him a weak smile that I knew wasn't at all pleasant, I said, "What else am I going to do? Wait for the vampire hunters to just decide they're tired of hunting the guys, and everything is just going to go back to normal?"

Darren just stared at me.

I huffed. "I'm tired of waiting. I'm tired of just sitting here and letting the hunters dictate our lives. Aren't you?"

"Why you?" Darren took a step into the bathroom and stopped. "You haven't been in our world long enough to know what you're getting into. You're just going to end up getting yourself killed."

Turning my back on him, I muttered, "I don't see you stepping up to do it. Now get out. I need to soak."

"I hope you know what you're doing." Darren lingered for a moment longer before leaving, closing the door behind him.

When he was gone, I disrobed and sank into the tub, each burning inch, making my eyes water. I sighed heavily. "So do I. So do I."

Chapter 16

Darren

SITTING AT MY DESK in the hotel room, my eyes going crossed from looking over the numbers, I sighed heavily.

Thankfully, my phone rang, giving me an excuse to take a break.

Lifting the phone to my ear without checking the number, I answered, "Hello, Master Durand."

Rayne's young voice came over the speaker. "Where's Piper?"

Well, hello to you too, I thought. Out loud, I answered, "Piper is still at her day job. May I take a message?"

Rayne growled over the phone. "No. Why are you letting her work anyway? Don't we pay you all enough?"

Holding back another sigh, I replied, "Of course, Master Durand. And as well as you know, stopping Piper from doing anything she puts her mind to is near impossible."

Rayne cursed under his breath and chuckled. "Ain't that the fucking truth." He huffed and then bit out, "Just tell her I'll be there soon. I don't want to waste any of the time we have with her working the whole time."

"Of course, Master Durand. I will pass on the message." I kept my voice even and without emotion.

"Good." The phone went dead.

Setting my phone down, I shook my head and sighed. No working while he was here. Ha. That was going to be fun to explain. I couldn't even get her to listen to me when it was for her own good.

For the last month, Piper has come home aching and wincing in pain. I felt helpless. Unable to help her. Unable to convince her to stop this madness.

Martial arts.

Bah.

What did Piper think she was going to accomplish by abusing her body this way? It certainly wouldn't do anything against the vampire hunters. They'd shoot her all the same.

I was tempted to tell Antoine about Piper's new 'hobby.' However, when I mentioned it to Piper, she begged me not to tell. I didn't like it, but it made her feel better. So, I'd sit back and let her come home with bruises that made me tense and take ice baths that were on the verge of giving her hypothermia.

For now.

I tried to turn back to my work, but my heart just wasn't in it. Rayne was going to be here any time now, and I'd have to make myself scarce. I didn't believe for a second that Rayne would be as welcoming as Antoine had been. I had no designs on Rayne's self. Still, I doubted he'd see my wish to be included as anything other than a challenge to his relationship with Piper.

The scent of berries hit my nose, and I sat up straighter in my chair, shifting uncomfortably in the jeans I'd taken to wearing. I'd have changed back to my usual attire for my sake. However, it was worth the discomfort for the way Piper's eyes trailed after me every time I left the room. I had an ass that didn't quit apparently—her words, not mine.

I twisted in my seat to face the door as it opened. Piper came in still dressed in her work attire. Odd for a Thursday.

Brows drawn together, I watched her enter the room, throwing her bag and coat onto a nearby chair. I'd given up trying to get her to put her things away. Now, I just picked up after her when she was gone.

When her eyes landed on me, my whole body tightened with anticipation. Piper's tongue darted out to wet her lips involuntarily, her eyes skimming over my form. Her scent had changed. Just a subtle change, but it was enough to make my length go stiff.

Those pale brown eyes finally landed on my face, and an excited grin spread across her face. "Hard day at work?"

"In a way." I tapped the desk with my bare hand, my white gloves put away neatly in my drawer. Piper had hounded me about them ever since I changed my clothing.

"They don't go with your outfit. How are you going to explain them to people?"

I hadn't planned to explain myself at all to the citizens of Seabrick. I didn't owe them any explanation. However, Piper seemed obsessed with getting them off, and as if she were my master, I had an overwhelming urge to please her.

"No class today?" I asked as she went into the bathroom.

Through the closed door, she called, "No, I went to check something else out today."

That had me up and out of my seat. Leaning against the wall by the bathroom door, I probed her almost gleefully, "Giving up already?"

Piper snorted, and the bathroom door opened abruptly. "Hell no. But I do have a surprise for you."

Her grin was contagious, and I found myself smiling despite myself. "A surprise?"

Nodding in a jerking motion, Piper grabbed my hand and pulled me toward the door. "Come on. We can grab something to eat afterward."

Unable or perhaps unwilling to argue with her, I allowed Piper to lead me out of the hotel room and down the hallway until we were out on the street. Out on the sidewalk, her hand slid down my arm and laced her fingers with mine.

I swallowed thickly. Too afraid to mention it in case Piper didn't mean to do it.

We walked hand in hand down the street with Piper a step ahead of me the whole time. Finally, we stopped.

I glanced away from Piper and realized we were in front of a house. I hadn't been paying any mind to where we were going, my attention had been completely absorbed with the woman before me.

"What do you think?" She released my hand, not at all self-conscious about it, going to stand in front of the house.

I turned toward her and scanned over the pale green house. It was quaint. Not even close to as big as the manor but still a good size all the same. There were bushes and big trees in the front yard. A picket fence surrounded the house, and a path led around the back toward the beach. The windows were big and full, allowing an abundance of natural light to filter into it when it was daytime. Right now, the evening light lay softly on the horizon.

Returning my gaze to Piper, I frowned. "It's nice. Why are we here?"

Piper practically vibrated as she beamed at me. "It's mine!"

My brows scrunched together. "Yours? How could it be-"

"I bought it," Piper interrupted, grabbing my hand again and bringing me over to the window. "Today. After work. I filled out the paperwork, and in thirty days, we'll move out of that drab hotel room and into a real house. No more having to eat out all the time. No more fighting for space." She wrapped her arms around me and squeezed tight. "Isn't it fantastic?"

Placing my arms around her, I found myself saying, "Yes, it is."

Piper lifted her head up, her eyes peering into mine. There was so much happiness there it made my chest tight. Her expression softened as we stared down at each other. Shifting in my arms, she pushed up closer to me, her eyes flickering to my lips.

I lowered my head to meet her.

"Why isn't this just a cozy situation?"

Chapter 17

Piper

I JERKED MY HEAD in the direction of the voice. My gaze shot over to where Rayne stood by the fence. His eyes narrowed, and his chest heaved as if he had been running. Which was pointless since vampires didn't need to breathe.

"Rayne," I breathed, not pushing away from Darren, but giving the vampire my full attention. "I didn't know you were coming today."

Rayne glowered at Darren. "Apparently, I need to have a talk with the help about passing along messages."

I turned my attention back to Darren.

Darren stood stiff in my arms but didn't back down from Rayne. It was one of the first times I'd ever seen him not grovel at their feet when something went wrong. His voice came out polite and yet void of any emotion. It was a lie. Underneath my hands, he practically vibrated with anger. "I was unaware of when you would arrive, Master Durand." He said master as if it were something vile in his mouth he had to spit out. "I hadn't had the chance to pass along your message as of yet."

One minute Rayne was by the gate, and the next, he was by our side. His hand wrapped in the front of Darren's shirt, jerking him away from me. "It looks like you had enough time to get cozy with *my* girlfriend. I'd say you had enough time to tell her, but chose not to."

Eyes widening, I tried to get between them. Pushing at Rayne's shoulder, I cried, "That's enough, Rayne. Put him down."

Rayne angled his head toward me, his red hair falling into his face but he didn't release Darren. "Darren needs to remember where his place is."

I narrowed my eyes on him. "And where exactly is that?"

"He's a servant. Nothing but the hired help. He should act that way." Rayne snarled, his fangs flashing.

Pain and anger pierced my chest, and I was sure it showed on my face. "Is that all I am to you then? The hired help? I can't be your girlfriend and lower than you, Rayne. You can't have it both ways." I tried once more to push between them. Why wasn't Darren fighting back? Why would he just take this kind of treatment? "I mean it, Rayne. Let him go. What I do with Darren is my business."

"And what would Antoine think about *your* business?" Rayne shot back.

I tried my best to keep my mind blank, but I had a hard time keeping myself from shooting back that Antoine would have been dandy with it, seeing as he already screwed us both. I didn't need to let Rayne see that night in my head.

"That's none of your business either." I crossed my arms over my chest but felt the heat build on my face.

"Oh, so you're cheating on me now?" Rayne scowled, dropping Darren abruptly.

Darren stumbled back more gracefully than I ever would have.

Rayne stared at me for a long moment, and then his eyes widened. He took a step back from us, his gaze darting between us. "Antoine never said anything. He never even thought about it."

"Well," I started and shrugged, refusing to be embarrassed about it, "now you know."

Rayne swallowed audibly and pointed a finger between Darren and me. "Are you two..." He cleared his throat. "Are you together-together then?"

I peeked over at Darren. His face was unreadable. Were we? I didn't know. Why didn't Darren say something? Don't leave this all up to me.

After a moment, when Darren didn't step forward to say anything, I answered, my heart aching the whole time. "No. It was a onetime thing."

Rayne frowned, his brows drawn tightly as he focused on Darren.

What did Rayne see in Darren's head? I wanted nothing more than for him to share it with me, but I couldn't ask that. It was the worst invasion of privacy one could ever ask. Instead, I forced a small smile and stepped toward Rayne.

"Now that that's out of the way," I wrapped my arms around Rayne's neck and kissed him. He didn't kiss me back right away. When Rayne began to respond, I pulled back, ending the kiss. "I missed you."

Rayne's lips tugged to one side. "I missed you too."

"Let's get out of here, yeah?" I glanced over my shoulder at Darren. "I'll see you later, alright?"

Darren nodded his head and said nothing once more.

I led Rayne away, pushing down the way my heart had seemed to force itself into my throat. The entire time I felt Darren's eyes on my back as we left.

Chapter 18

Darren

IN THE DURAND HOUSE, we never bothered with a Christmas tree or even celebrating the holiday. Boris, the Durands' sire, made every holiday an excuse to play his games of torture and deceit. He wanted to see just how far he could push his underlings, and it ruined all the holidays for us from then on.

Piper had brought the tradition back.

"Hand me that green one." Piper reached back behind her, pointing at the box next to me. She stood on a ladder placing the ornaments on the tree she had insisted we buy. It filled the moderate-sized living room until there was barely any room to maneuver.

I found the green ornament and lifted it up so she could reach it.

She took it from my hand, making sure not to touch me in the process.

It had been like this since Rayne. Since I'd kept my mouth shut and ruined everything. I held back a sigh. Every step forward I made with Piper ended up being three steps back because of my insecurities.

If I had just said something, anything, when Rayne asked, then maybe we would be doing this together rather than robotic-like as if I weren't really here.

Rayne had seen inside of my head. He knew what I felt for Piper, and yet he kept his mouth shut. It made me thankful and resentful toward him. Rayne was one of the only members of the Durand that had a power that I truly disliked. People's thoughts were private, and they should stay that way.

"I need a red one now," Piper said, jerking me out of my thoughts.

Grabbing a red ornament from the box, I held it out to her. This time her attention was on the tree, and our fingers brushed ever so slightly. Piper startled and jerked her hand back as if burned. The ornament dropped between us, shattering on the floor.

"Shit." Piper started down the steps, her short shorts clinging to her lovely butt. It might be December, but in southern Georgia, the weather was only mild. Nothing like the winters in Germany where the cold was so biting that you couldn't breathe, and you'd be lucky to see a neck, let alone the curve of someone's backside. My gaze lingered on Piper's luscious cheeks peeking out from beneath her shorts, and my body flushed with need.

I cleared my throat and darted for the kitchen. "I'll get a broom."

The more time I spent around Piper, the more I wanted her. The one taste with Antoine hadn't been enough. I wanted to kiss her. To hold her. To feel her writhing beneath me. Unfortunately, unless something changed, none of those things were going to happen.

"Here," I tapped her knee where she was crouched by the glass fragments. "Let me."

Piper glanced up at me, some unreadable emotion in her eyes. A second later, the look changed to pain. "Ouch. Fuck." She lifted her hand, and a tiny bead of blood welled up on her pointer finger.

Setting the broom down, I reached for her hand. "Let me see." She hesitated before relenting, offering me her hand. Gently, I held her hand in mine, peering into the cut. "I don't see any glass."

"That's good, I guess." Piper huffed and began to pull her hand away. I held on, and Piper's mouth turned down at the edges.

Locking eyes with her, I did something so out of character for myself that I hardly believed I had done it. I lifted her injured finger to my mouth. I almost held my breath, expecting her to jerk her hand back from me. Still, Piper only watched in confusion and minute fascination.

Sliding her finger into my mouth, I sucked on the injury until the blood stopped flowing. I was not a lover of blood, but to have a piece of Piper inside of me, even such a small drop of blood made my heart beat faster. Piper swallowed audibly, licking her lips. She didn't move away from me or cry foul, which I supposed was something.

Piper took a half step forward and then seemed to think better of herself. She shook her head and withdrew her hand, brushing past me into the kitchen. "This better not get infected."

I laughed bitterly to myself. "We're going to live basically forever, and you're worried about an infection."

"Of course," Piper called from the kitchen, the sink turning on. "I don't want to lose my finger."

Opening my mouth to answer her, the doorbell rang. "I'll get it."

I strode over to the front door, glancing into the small window before opening it. Giving a slight bow, I greeted, "Master Durand, we weren't expecting you for a few days."

Drake's large muscular form pushed inside without invitation. "I got restless. Nice place." He shot a look around the house Piper and I had made into a home. "Where's my girl?"

A snort of disgust came from the kitchen doorway. "What am I, your property?"

Drake grinned and, in the blink of an eye, had Piper up and in his arms. "There she is." He kissed her loudly on the mouth. "Did you miss me?"

Piper giggled and pushed at his chest. "No. Now put me down."

"I don't believe you." Drake shook his head. "Tell me you missed me, and I'll put you down."

Closing the door, I locked it and went back to the tree where the glass ornament still needed cleaning.

"I will not." Piper snapped back and grunted. "I'm going to kick your ass if you don't put me down right now, Drake."

I paused, dropping the broom. Taking purposeful steps toward them, I grabbed Drake by the shoulder. Surprised by my intervention, Drake's eyes widened. "She said to let her go."

Drake frowned and then smirked. "Or what? You're going to kick my ass? You've never lifted a finger against us no matter what we do."

I didn't argue with him. It was true. I'd stood aside and let the Durands do what they wanted to do. Never before had any of their actions affected me, made me want to stop them. I was just Antoine's human servant, I didn't have the power or the abilities to stop them, even if I wanted to.

Now, even though I knew he wouldn't really hurt her, the fact that he was doing something to upset her, I couldn't stand by and watch. I just couldn't.

My hand tightened on his shoulder. The muscles beneath my hand barely twitched. "I will not ask you again, Draconius."

Now Drake did laugh. "Well, I'll be damned. Our girl has finally won over little Darren's ice-cold heart. Are you going to fight me for her? Huh? Are you?"

The fingers of my free hand curled into a fist, and I tensed prepared to go against one of my masters for the first time since I was saved in that infirmary. Prepared to ruin everything for one thing...her.

I didn't get the chance, though.

Piper jerked in Drake's arms. Drake's face contoured in pain, and he released Piper, grabbing at himself between his legs. When she got loose, Piper's fist swung out and caught Drake across the back of the head.

"Shit, Piper!" Drake grabbed his head and his genitals at the same time. "I need both of those heads. You need both of those heads."

I tried to keep my face neutral, but it was hard. My lips ticked with the effort.

Snorting, Piper shoved away from Drake and came to stand by me. "Right now, I don't want either of them. You're being a dick, and I don't appreciate being manhandled."

"You didn't seem to mind it last time." Drake shot back with a smirk and a wince. "Geez, when did your bite become worse than your bark?"

"Maybe when I got stuck waiting for your sorry asses." Piper glanced at me, and she must have seen something on my face because she smiled, winking. "Now, if you want to stay, you owe Darren and me an apology."

"Wait a second." Drake finally stood back up, his hands in front of him. "I know I pushed you too far, but why do I have to apologize to him?"

Piper laced her fingers through mine, startling me, but I didn't say anything. "Because I said so."

Drake scowled and seemed like he wasn't going to do it before he finally opened his mouth and grumbled a halfhearted, "Sorry."

"For?" Piper prompted.

Rolling his eyes, Drake huffed. "For being a dick. To both of you. Now can I stay?"

Piper grinned up at me. "What do you think, Darren? Can Drake stay?"

I allowed my lips to curl up finally, peering down at her. "Yes. I think Master Durand can stay. This time."

Chapter 19

Piper

ALLISTER DIDN'T SHOW UP in January for his appointment. There was no call. No explanation. Just nothing.

It made me feel helpless. Useless.

"Damn it." I hung up the phone again after the millionth call to Antoine, to Rayne, to Wynn, all the way down the line to fucking Marcus. None of them answered the phone.

"Calm down." Darren smoothed his hand over the back of my neck, massaging the tense muscles there. "This doesn't mean anything. Maybe they're not in a place with cell service? Or maybe they're hiding?"

"You don't know that." I stood from the couch and pushed his hands away. My heart raced in my chest, and my eyes burned with tears. "You can say all the theories you want, but you don't actually know. Neither of us does." I jerked the hand holding my phone to the side. "The link that connects us to Antoine doesn't work two ways. He can feel what we are feeling but not the other way around. He knows I'm upset." I hit my chest hard enough to sting. "Here. If he loved me. If any of them loved me and knew what I was feeling right now, wouldn't they come running? Shouldn't they?" The tears streamed down my face, wracking sobs made it hard to talk, hard to breathe.

I barely registered the fact that Darren had moved until his arms wrapped around me, rocking me gently in his embrace. He made shushing sounds as if I were a baby who needed comforting.

Burying my face in his chest, my phone made a thud as it hit the ground. My fingers twisted themselves into his shirt, holding him tightly against me. Darren stroked my hair in slow, soft motions, over and over, murmuring against the top of my head words I didn't understand.

Finally, when I could breathe again, I lifted my head to meet his gaze. "Is that Italian?"

Darren's lip quirked up at the side. "You have a good ear. Many don't recognize it. Or think it's French."

I giggled and sniffed. "I had an Italian boyfriend once. His grandmother used to yell at him in their language over family dinners. I didn't know you were Italian." I stared up into those deep dark brown eyes, noticing features about him I hadn't before. "I guess I don't know a whole lot about you."

Darren gave a noncommittal shrug. "There isn't a lot to know. My life is not, was not, that impressive."

"And yet, you somehow ended up here with me." I fiddled with his shirt, not meeting his eyes. "Did you ever expect that to happen?"

Shaking his head, Darren leaned forward and pressed a kiss to my forehead. "Nothing with you is ever expected. I've come to love that about you."

"You have?" I peeked up at him, feeling my face heat. "You don't think I'm just a big pain in the ass you wish you'd have thrown out the day we met?"

Darren threw his head back and laughed. "I used to think that, yes."

"But not anymore." I murmured, shuffling my feet closer to him, my eyes drawn to the curve of his lips.

"No," Darren answered, his voice just as low as mine. "Not anymore."

Licking my lips, I flicked my eyes up to his briefly. "What do you think of me now?"

Darren's hands drifted down to my waist, pressing our bodies against one another. "Now, I think you're still a pain in the ass."

I scoffed and smacked him on the chest, pulling back from him. Darren held me closer, a hand coming up to cup the side of my face. My breath caught.

"But I also think you're the most courageous, smart-mouthed," he grinned slightly, "beautiful woman I've ever met."

I blushed, ducking my eyes down. "Darren. You're just trying to make me feel better."

His thumb traced the line of my lower lip, tempting me to lick it again. "I keep telling myself you're not mine. I can't have you. You belong to the Durands." He took a deep breath, and I thought he was going to step away from me, but he didn't. Instead, he muttered, "Fuck the Durands," as his mouth descended on mine.

Darren's mouth devoured mine as if he wanted to climb inside of me. His teeth nipped at my lips, his tongue lashed against mine, each movement drove my desire for him higher and higher.

My hands pulled at the t-shirt he'd tucked into his jeans. I escaped his kiss long enough to command, "Off."

Grabbing the bottom of his shirt, Darren whipped it over his head, tossing it where it may.

I grinned, running my hands up his chest. "You're just going to leave that there?"

The warm press of Darren's hand slid beneath my shirt, playing along the edge of my pants. "I'll get it later."

I kissed him again, biting his lower lip before asking, "You sure? It isn't killing you right now?"

Darren slid his hands down my waist and over the curve of my butt, pulling me against him so I could feel how hard he was beneath his jeans. "Not as much as something else is right now." He kissed me once more, cupping my thighs and lifting me up. I wrapped my legs around him, holding on tightly as he walked us through the house and toward the bedroom.

We paused in the hallway to take my shirt off. Darren didn't paw me like most men would have, he gazed down at the tops of my breasts like a man dying of thirst but too polite to ask for it.

"Touch me," I whispered into the darkened hallway. When he didn't move right away, I reached behind me and undid my bra. I threw it to the side, exposing my breast to him. Darren's gaze ate up my bare skin, and still, he didn't touch me.

I pressed my chest against him, rubbing my nipples along his warm flesh. "If you can't touch my breasts, then what I plan to happen next is going to be a bit hard."

Darren chuckled. "And what do you expect to happen?"

I leaned back from him, arching a brow. "If the position we're in doesn't tell you, then

I don't know what you've been doing with Antoine, but it's not sex."

"Oh, no. Believe me, what Antoine does is nothing like this." Darren slid his hands over my ass and then back down my thighs. "He'd never let me be in so much control."

I snorted. "You too, huh?"

Grinning slightly, Darren's eyes dipped to my chest. "I won't grope you like a teenage boy in the hallway. You deserve more than that. You deserve adoration, a bed, and time. Lots of time."

I wiggled in his arms. "Then giddy up, *signore*. This sauce needs your noodle."

Darren arched a brow at me and then laughed, shaking his head. "Did you just try and make an Italian pun? Because that was horrible."

Shrugging, I looped my arms around his shoulders. "I don't know any sexy Italian innuendos. Sue me."

He said something in Italian too fast for me to understand, but I understood one word. *Scoparti.* My ex-boyfriend had said that enough to me to know what it meant. Fuck you and not in the insulting sense.

I leaned my head back to meet his gaze. "What was that?"

Darren grinned. "I'll show you."

Finally, Darren lifted me away from the wall and walked us to the bedroom. He lowered me to the bed and knelt between my thighs. Darren's dark head bent over me, murmuring Italian against my skin. His mouth skimmed over my neck, burning all the way down to my chest. His fingers brushed against the curve of my breasts, his tongue wet and warm circled around my nipple before encasing it in his mouth. My back arched against his face, pushing my chest further into his mouth.

Lacing my fingers into his hair, I tugged on it until he released my nipple with a pop. "Later. Adore me later. Fuck me now."

Darren chuckled. The sound of it all male, the only way men did it when they were thinking about sex. It made things low inside of me tighten, and grow wet. Well, wetter.

Sliding his hands from my breasts, he trailed them down my stomach and along the edge of my pants. Like an old pro, he flicked my pants open, unzipped them, and had them and my panties halfway down my legs before I knew what was happening.

"Someone's had practice," I breathed as my hot center was exposed to the cool air of the room.

Darren lowered his mouth to my hip bone, dragging his mouth along the bone. "Decades of practice."

My hips jerked at one spot, and he did it again. "Darren. Please."

"Oh, I like that." Darren's lips curled against me, lifting his eyes. "Do it again."

Usually, I'd have argued the fact, but my body burned too hot to stop, and I'd do just about anything to get him inside of me now. "Please, Darren. No more teasing."

"What do you want?"

I threw my head back and growled, "Ugh, you fucking men. You can't just fuck me. You have to make me say it." I looked down at him, my brows drawn. "I want you to take your pants off and fuck me until I can't see straight. Clear enough?"

"Yes," Darren breathed as if something in him could finally relax. Pulling away from me, he removed his own pants as quickly as he did mine. When Darren came back to me, he cupped my arms, lifting me up against him before sliding inside of me without even having to look. Practice, he'd said. It made me wonder briefly how much practice he'd had, but then Darren was moving, and I couldn't think of anything else but the back of my eyelids.

"Fuck. Fuck." Darren murmured into my ear, thrusting against me once more. "You feel...oh...fuck."

I never expected Darren to be so talkative during sex. He hadn't been the last two times we'd been intimate. Maybe it was something to do with Antoine since he was there both times.

Unfortunately, my brain was turning into pasta, and I couldn't overthink it now.

I was just on the cusp of an orgasm when the house phone we had in case of emergencies rang.

Darren paused mid-thrust.

"Don't you dare stop." I gasped, shifting my hips against him. "They didn't answer my calls. They can damn well leave a message."

"Could be important." Darren stared through the wall as if he could see through it to the kitchen where the phone sat.

"So's this," I gripped his ass with my hands, my nails digging into his flesh as I urged him further inside of me.

The answering machine finally picked up.

"Hey, it's me." Allister's voice came through the walls muffled but there. "We had to ditch the phones. I'll be coming around in a couple of days." There was a pause and talking that I couldn't pick up before Allister said, "My brother says to stop worrying so much. See you soon. Everyone sends their love. Bye."

"See?" Darren peered down at me with a soft smile. "Nothing to worry about."

I squeezed his ass once more. "I'm not worried. Were you worried?"

Laughing, Darren mercifully began to move once more. I gasped as he hit something deep inside of me, our bodies swaying and rocking with each other. I closed my eyes tight against the onslaught of pleasure, my head tilted back as I moaned.

"Look at me, Piper," Darren commanded, lifting a hand to my face. "See me. I want to know you are thinking of me while I'm right here," he thrust hard enough to bring a gasp from my throat, "inside of you. No one else."

"Oh, I couldn't forget." I breathed out, wrapping my legs around his waist. "Now show me what those extra muscles you've been hiding can do."

"It is my pleasure to serve you, Miss Billings," Darren smirked at me, before he picked up the pace, shifting his angle so that he hit the spot inside of me over and over again until I was falling to pieces beneath him. Darren came shortly after me, grunting as he stilled in my arms before collapsing next to me on the mattress.

"You know," I said, curled up next to him. "You technically are a Durand."

Darren kissed my shoulder. "So? My words still stand true."

I giggled. "Yeah. I guess you're right." I shifted closer to him, pulling my lower lip into my mouth. "So, want to stick it to the Durands one more time?"

Chuckling, Darren leaned in to kiss me. "Only one?"

Pressing my mouth to his, I murmured, "I suppose I could do it a few more times. One for each of them."

Darren smiled against my mouth. "Sounds like a plan to me."

Chapter 20
Piper

WAKING UP NEXT TO someone was strange, to say the least. I'd never actually slept with any of the Durands. I mean, I've slept, but they didn't. So, waking up and rolling over to find a warm body next to me was a bit jolting.

Darren slept like everything else he did. Perfect.

He didn't snore. He didn't hog the covers. In fact, I'd almost say he was dead had his chest not been moving up and down with his breath. Slowly, I shifted off the bed and slipped into my clothing. Tying the robe, I walked through my bedroom and toward the living room area.

Heading to the kitchen, I grabbed a mug off the counter and flicked on the coffee pot. While the pot worked, I leaned against the counter and just waited. It was strange how content I was right now, just being here and not at the hotel. I almost never wanted to leave. Almost.

When the coffee was done, I filled my cup with cream and sugar and went into the living room. I curled up into a chair by the window and watched the street, sipping my coffee.

How had I not known what was right in front of me all along?

Oh, I know.

That was an easy one.

I was blinded by the beauty of the Durands and the mask Darren put up between us. I wondered briefly what would have happened if I had fallen for Darren first? Would I still have gotten with the rest of them?

The only imperfection I could find in the man in the other room was how long it took him to make a move. Though, I supposed it was hard to change who you are after decades of doing whatever your master tells you to. I wasn't really one to talk. I had so many men in my life adding another one would only complicate matters more.

All I knew was, I couldn't imagine giving any of them up. Not now. Not ever.

The vampire hunters were just going to have to live with missing out on this one because I wasn't giving up that easily. If Antoine and the others couldn't figure this out, then I guess it was up to me to fix it.

Billy said I was ready to move onto weapons training now. I had to be at one with my body and mind before I could add an extension on to it. Or some bullshit like that. A part of me was frightened of what was to come, and the other part couldn't wait.

I guess I never was quite suited for desk work. I'd always been more of a woman of action. And I was about to get all the action I could ever ask for. I only hoped that I was ready for it.

About the Author

Erin Bedford is an otaku, recovering coffee addict, and Legend of Zelda fanatic. Her brain is so full of stories that need to be told that she must get them out or explode into a million screaming chibis. Obsessed with fairy tales and bad boys, she hasn't found a story she can't twist to match her deviant mind full of innuendos, snarky humor, and dream guys.

On the outside, she's a work from home mom and bookbinger. One the inside, she's a thirteen-year-old boy screaming to get out and tell you the pervy joke they found online. As an ex-computer programmer, she dreams of one day combining her love for writing and college credits to make the ultimate video game!

Until then, when she's not writing, Erin is devouring as many books as possible on her quest to have the biggest book gut of all time. She's written over thirty books, ranging from paranormal romance, urban fantasy, and even scifi romance.

Come chat me up!
www.erinbedford.com
Facebook.com/erinrbedford
twitter.com/erin_bedford